Casey

Casey

An American Extreme Bull Riders Tour Romance

Kelly Hunter

TULE
PUBLISHING

Casey

Copyright © 2017 Kelly Hunter
Tule Publishing First Printing, May 2017
The Tule Publishing Group, LLC

ALL RIGHTS RESERVED

No part of this book may be used or reproduced in any manner whatsoever without written permission except in the case of brief quotations embodied in critical articles and reviews.

This is a work of fiction. Names, characters, places, and incidents are products of the author's imagination or are used fictitiously. Any resemblance to actual events, locales, organizations, or persons, living or dead, is entirely coincidental.

ISBN: 978-1-946772-64-0

Rowan Harper has traveled the *American Extreme Bull Riders* tour circuit with her stock-contractor father since she was four years old. She's seen the best rides and the worst wrecks. And then there's T.J. who impressed her mightily when he didn't ride at all.

Tomas James Casey walked away from his rightful place in last year's bull-riding finals in order to bury his father. His sponsors are gone, but he's back to stake his claim. He wants the buckle, sure, but he also wants the woman he can't stop thinking about.

Can T.J. really score the championship and the girl? Or will he have to choose between the two … once and for all?

Chapter One

"WELL, NOW. IF it isn't the part-time cowboy, back to show us how it's done."

Tomas James Casey took his eyes off the activity around the back of the chutes long enough to spare a glance for the man who'd lit up next to him. The words could have been read as an insult, except for the genuine smile coming from the man who'd said them.

Paulo Contreras was a wiry, bandy-legged bull rider whose friendly smile hid a heart that never gave up. He was a regular on the American Extreme Bull Riders tour and one of the few who'd ever offered Casey a hand, advice or an in with the select group of riders that toured year after year.

"Well, now, if it isn't the old man," Casey replied, as the other man slung himself lightly over the top rail of the fence and settled to sit beside him. "Good to see you too."

"You missed Vegas." Paulo's eyes held questions that mirrored his words. "Where were you, amigo?"

"My father took a fall and my mother needed me home."

"Did you mention you were within two hundred points of the lead and had a good chance of taking home a million-dollar paycheck and a world championship?"

"I mentioned it." And he'd felt like a heel the minute the words had left his mouth. Out of all four of his brothers, only one of them had backed his request to delay the funeral a few days so he could ride in the finals. The other three had shut him down hard, tempers running hot, and his mother had started crying on account of the shouting, and that had been the end of that. "It wasn't worth the family meltdown."

"So how is your father?" asked Paulo.

"Dead."

Paulo turned to eyeball him sharply. "You could have mentioned it."

"Telling you now." Casey smiled faintly. "Old news now."

He could talk about it now without the suffocating weight of sorrow rendering him speechless.

"You could have mentioned it *at the time*."

"I didn't want the AEBR promo machine making a meal out of it. Better off not telling anyone until it was all over."

"I'm surprised management let you back at all, with that attitude."

"Yeah." So was he. They hadn't exactly been bending over to welcome him. Miss an event without written medical cause and he was out. Be anything but their biddable promotions bitch this season and he was gone. Ride to win, stay in the top two dozen or he was gone. At least that last stipulation applied to everyone. "Extenuating circumstances."

"How's your mother?" Paulo asked after a couple of moments' contemplative silence.

"She has five sons all trying to step into boots they can never fill. I have it on good authority that we're driving her mad."

"Tour'll do you good, then."

"Reckon so."

Casey liked the life he led for the most part, and he flat-out loved the adrenaline rush that came with bull riding. Didn't even mind the travel, to an extent. He got to criss-cross the country, take in the sights and the sounds, and there was company when he wanted it and solitude when he didn't. There was the spectacle and the theater of the sport, and at the heart of it there were eight seconds between him and a bull and damn but he loved to win that argument. Focus on the ride and nothing else, and the points and the standings took care of themselves.

"Looks like the gang's all here." He could see the familiar Harper stock provider banner on one of the gates. He could see a woman working the pens behind the chutes, although at first glance she could be mistaken for a slender, half-grown boy. She was Joe Harper's only daughter and Joe was a retired bull-riding legend who'd won enough to set himself up to breed bucking bulls back in the days when that was nearly unheard of.

This was Casey's fifth year on the tour. He figured it for Rowan Harper's twentieth, given the rumor that her father had been carting her around various bull-riding circuits since she was four years old.

"You always look for her." Paulo had seen the direction of his gaze.

"She's interesting. Never seen anyone work harder than she does, man or woman." In Casey's humble opinion she was also the prettiest thing he'd ever seen, and that included all the models and promoters employed to work the bars and the merchandise kiosks.

She had short brown hair and big brown eyes. What little of her there was, she hid beneath baggy jeans and checkered men's shirts. Sometimes her hair reached the tips of her thin shoulders and other times it looked as if she'd taken to it with a pair of scissors and no mirror. She usually wore a cap with the Harper logo on it but today she simply wore sunglasses. And gloves. Those too.

Last year a girlfriend of one of the riders had commented on Rowan's rough hands and blunt nails and had pulled a laugh from the cowboys she'd been standing with. Rowan had been part of the group, and Casey hadn't been the only one to see the flash of hurt in her eyes, or the way she'd shoved her hands in her jeans pockets, offered a tight smile and excused herself shortly thereafter.

Leather gloves, the soft supple ones bull riders wore, had become a workwear staple for her after that.

"You need to stop looking in her direction," said Paulo next. "She doesn't look back."

"True enough." Except maybe once or twice, toward the end of last year, she'd looked his way and held his stare and started a fire in him that had never quite gone out. And now he *was* back, and this was his last tour, and maybe he was looking to take something other than memories and money with him when he left. "She sent me a phone message when my father was dying."

"She knew?"

"No. Well, not that I know of. She asked after me." Not where the hell are you or what do you think you're doing. No judgment at all and the lack of it had soothed him, calmed him more than he would have thought possible. "It was only three words."

"Did you write back?"

"And say what?"

"Something. Anything. No?"

No.

"So the woman you've spent the last, oh, let's say two years pining for reached out to you in your time of need and you didn't write back."

"I wanted a different kind of start." Not one wrapped in weakness and grief. He'd wanted something else to offer Rowan Harper but for all his sideways glances he was still none the wiser as to what she might *want*. "Do you think she has another life besides this one? One where she's not trying to be her father's son?"

Paulo adjusted his grip on the top rail and looked down

at the dirt, as if contemplating the unseen particles of the universe. "I know she took a bet in Deadwood one night nearly ten years back, after she chewed out a rookie for using his spurs wrong. To be fair, the guy didn't know squat and didn't last long. But she got into a pissing contest with him and the next minute they had one of her daddy's best bucking bulls in a chute and good money was going down as to whether or not she could show that rookie how it was done."

"Really?" Casey could appreciate a good story setup as well as the next man. "What happened?"

"Wasn't her rope, wasn't her glove, she wore the rookie's spurs, and someone a little smarter than the rest of them made her wear their vest. That someone might have been me. We had no other safety measures in place, no one else on the ground besides the half-dozen cowboys standing watch. Must've been three or four a.m. Full moon, no lights. Outdoor arena and a sweet summer night."

"Helmet?"

"No."

It was a setup for catastrophe. "And?"

"It was one of the most glorious ninety-five-point rides I've ever seen, I swear to God. Not the first time that girl had ridden her daddy's bulls, trust me."

"What'd her father say?"

"Can't say he was surprised. But three cowboys got suspended, the rest got fined—including yours truly—and

Harper almost lost his stock contract. You've never seen a man on such a tear. He put the fear of the devil into every last cowboy involved and then ripped his daughter a new one. There was talk about banning her for life only it was hard to make that stick seeing as they wanted Harper's bulls and he couldn't leave her at home because she was still underage and there was no one at home to see to her."

"What about her mother?"

"Harper's wife died in childbirth."

"Giving birth to Rowan?"

"Giving birth to a son who died at the same time the wife did."

"That's a horrible story, man."

"But it explains why Harper's girl keeps her head down, now don't it?"

It also explained why looking into Rowan Harper's eyes sometimes felt a lot like looking into a million miles of wet road. "Yeah, all right. Why doesn't she ride?"

"Well, now. That's a question for Rowan, her daddy, and the powers that shape this beautiful sport. It's not for lack of skill or training. I figure it for somewhere they don't want her to be."

"I'm going to ask her to dinner."

Paulo huffed a laugh. "Is this before or after you explain why you didn't reply to her?"

"Before." Hopefully that particular conversation would never come up. "That's what you do, right? You like someone; you ask them out."

"Around here, if you like the look of someone you buy them drinks after they've seen you ride. Then you invite them to stay a while at the end of the night and try to remember their name the next morning."

Casey had done that a time or two—there was no denying it. But those morning-afters had never sat well with him—too much hope in a woman's eye and never enough coffee. They wanted the fantasy, the extreme-sports athlete, not a man with a fresh pile of aches and bruises and a burning need for silence. "We both know that's not going to work with her."

"Neither's asking her out. Rowan doesn't date bull riders. Don't say I didn't warn you."

So much for friendly encouragement. Casey tried to push the other man off the fence but Paulo wasn't a bull rider for nothing and merely swayed before righting himself and shooting Casey a smartass grin.

"Mind standing my bulls for me this weekend?" Paulo asked next.

"Do the same for me and you've got a deal. Where's Huck?" Huck and Paulo usually stood each other's rides. Traveled together too, at times.

"Back in Kentucky with a shoulder injury, a newborn babe and a wife who's glad to see him. Doc says he needs to give it a month. I figure he'll be back in two weeks if he can get medical clearance."

Casey shook his head—didn't know what decision he'd make if he was in the same position. Bull riding could be good to a man if he stayed fit and healthy, covered his rides and stayed in the money.

Not everyone was that lucky.

SOME RIDERS LIKED to sit and watch in silence before it was their turn in the chute. Some ran their mouths and made bad jokes. Others had elaborate rituals and routines that you didn't want to get in the way of. Casey figured himself for yet another kind of cowboy—focused, but not so focused that he couldn't summon a laugh. Quiet, but not so silent that he couldn't speak when spoken to. Hungry for the ride—he was always that. Win or lose, the adrenaline hit that came with the ride made everything brighter, louder, and put a heat beneath his skin that made him want to peel out of it. He wasn't the only cowboy addicted to it.

Paulo was set to ride in the first half-dozen cowboys through the chutes. Casey had helped him in the chute enough times to know what Paulo wanted and when he wanted it. The show announcer's opening spiel had settled his nerves and reminded him that they were here to entertain and there was no better way to do that than play to the born-tough image, cover your bulls and be humble about it if you won.

The playbook varied a bit from rider to rider but that was the gist of it.

Paulo covered his bull with a solid ride and a score of eighty-two.

Casey rode his, and bounced off the dirt eight seconds later with a score of eighty-four. Not enough to put either of them in the lead but enough to be going on with. Paulo gutted out an eighty during his second ride, and Casey did two better again. When the draw came through the following morning, Casey was down to ride Harper's new bull *Over Easy* in the final round. No one had ridden the athletically unpredictable four-year-old yet and he figured it for the perfect excuse to seek Rowan out. They could talk about the bull and then casually, somewhere in the middle of it all, he'd ask her out and she'd realize she really did want to get to know him a whole lot better and say yes.

Given that he now had a game plan, it only made sense to head to the Jackson coliseum early rather than later. The big indoor arena had seating for around seven thousand and sometimes people could be hard to find.

Sometimes, but not always.

As usual, both Joe Harper and Rowan were in the thick of things. Casey watched and waited for a break in the work before approaching Rowan. He knew better than to offer to help. Joe Harper—three time stock contractor of the year—rarely had much to say but when he did talk it paid to listen, and his yearly greeting to riders never varied. *You don't touch my bulls until you're on their backs. If they don't stand for you, a Harper employee will come and fix that. Once the gate opens, good luck.*

Finally, Rowan penned the last of the load and made her way toward him. He figured she'd known he was there for a while. It helped that he'd planted himself along the run where they brought the bulls in from outside.

"Hello, stranger," she said when finally she stood beside him. "Heard you were back."

"Not you too." He'd been copping flak all weekend for having bailed on the finals last year. Everything from the announcers calling him a part-time cowboy to former fans not bothering to acknowledge his rides. There was judgment in Rowan's voice too. "And here I thought you'd be happy to see me. It's good to see you," he offered, and it was. Up close, he could see the smattering of freckles across her nose and the luxurious sweep of black eyelashes over warm brown eyes. "I missed you."

"Where were you?"

It was as if she hadn't heard the compliment. Or hadn't taken it as such.

"My father had money on you taking the buckle last year," she continued. "He wasn't too pleased when you didn't show for your final rides."

"Did you have money on me too?"

"Good to know your ego's still alive and well."

Although not for long if she had her way.

She studied him frankly, as if he was a puzzle piece she couldn't place. "I definitely thought you were in with a chance," she said finally. "You let a lot of fans down. I hear you lost sponsors too."

Yeah, well. That was a sore point. "I was needed at home so I went. I'm not a part-time cowboy, no matter what people think, but I do put family first. No exceptions. Now are you going to come out to dinner with me or what?"

"What?"

He probably could have used a better lead-in and a whole lot less *element of surprise.*

"Dinner. Tonight. After the show."

"Assuming you're still standing," she said dryly. "You drew our best bull."

"So I hear. Do you really call him *Eggs* for short?"

"Why? You don't like it?" She smiled and went from being merely beautiful to utterly breathtaking in an instant. "It doesn't have quite the same ring as *Trainwreck* or *Hammerfall,* but I like to think his gentle name suits him well enough. Until someone tries to ride him. As for your other question, I don't date bull riders."

"I heard that."

"And promptly took it as a challenge. I'm disappointed in you, Tomas James. You're the fourth cowboy who's tried to pick me up so far this tour. Granted, you're the only sober one, but my answer's the same. I'm not your meal ticket when it comes to getting off a bull's back and into the heady world of stock contracting. I'm not any man's trophy, besides which I don't tend to look the part. I don't want to rehash your best five rides over the entree, although I could probably tell you what they were. And if you're after information on how *I* think the bull you're about to ride is going to buck and how best you should ride him for maximum points, all you have to do is ask. I'll tell anyone that. Not that anyone does ask."

"So that was a no to dinner?"

"You're very smart."

He got that a lot. Smartass. Book smart. Too smart for his own good. He was the only one of five boys who'd ever gone to college. Give his opinion on a family ranching decision these days and he'd be accused of being a clueless college intellectual—as if he didn't also have the practical experience everyone else at the table had.

"Rowan, I've got four brothers and they're all older, bar one. Put-downs are not a deterrent. They're like a little taste of home. Now, if you ask any of my brothers, bar one, whether their put-downs have any effect at all, they're likely to tell you it does nothing but make me dig in."

"And what does your bar-one brother say?" The tiniest of smiles now graced her perfect lips—lips that were full and plump, not too wide, and shaped to mimic the curve of her jaw and chin.

"Do I have something on my face?" she asked, and wiped her gloved hand across her mouth before he could answer either question.

Well, she did *now*.

"Little bit of dirt, right there." He showed her on his own face by rubbing at a spot to one side of his lips. "As for my younger brother, he'd say he can deflate me easy enough, and he can. I've no intention of introducing him to you for a very long time. I can picture you learning all his bad habits."

Her smile came at him a little faster this time. "Much as I like the sound of your family dynamics, I'm still not having dinner with you."

"If I ask you how you think I should go about riding *Eggs Benedict* over there and then stick it for eight seconds … will you have dinner with me then?"

"What is this, a bet?"

"It's kind of a bet. What's your advice on the ride?"

"My guess is the bull will start with more air than you can handle and break left, away from your hand. Ride him left-handed, you ambidextrous wonder, keep your left leg set, rake with your right, and you might stay on longer than most. Once he switches direction—and he will—you're toast. Try not to get hung up."

"Bold advice, Ro. Do you have any idea how often I botch the dismount when I ride left-handed?"

"Forty-one percent of the time over the past two years. It's a lot, but it's still your best bet for this ride. Assuming you want to stay on longer than three seconds."

Casey blinked. "How do you know that? I don't even

know that."

"I'm here. I get bored. I run the math. What else is there to do?"

"We really need to get you some hobbies. You can tell me what else you're interested in over dinner. Besides me."

"Don't get too smug, cowboy. I can tell you those kinds of stats on everyone. I've got a little book."

"And I wouldn't mind getting a look at it."

"Get your own."

He offered up his most charming smile. The one that so rarely let him down once he chose to use it. "But, Ro, yours is already done. You could be my mentor. My trainer. My secret weapon. I've always wanted a secret weapon. Four brothers and not a moment's peace. I used to dream of secret weapons."

She smiled back as if she couldn't help it.

"Is that a yes?" he pushed. "You'll take the bet? If I cover *Over Easy* we'll go out for a meal?"

"I don't celebrate with cowboys after the event. I load up; I'm gone."

"Where will you be tomorrow, lunchtime?"

"All going well, I'll be several hours east of Jackson and heading for Montgomery with a truck full of bulls."

"I can meet you on the road. It's pretty country. We can have a picnic."

"You're mad."

"Surely this isn't news, given my occupation. Or we

could catch a meal in Atlanta. I'm not going home between now and then." Too far south for returning to Montana to be anything but foolish. "I'll come in early. You're always early." They had a week to fill between here and Atlanta, and although he didn't exactly know what Rowan's plans involved, he did know there were a lot of hours to fill between one event and the next.

A shout from the rear end of the laneway warned of another bull heading toward them. Rowan raised her hand and opened the gate before climbing the rail and getting out of the way. Casey followed suit.

"All right," she said, not even looking at him. "If you can cover my bull, riding the way I said to, I'll eat with you. I'll even bring my little book of facts and figures."

So much for Rowan Harper not dating cowboys. That or she figured he had no chance in hell of riding that bull. "Have you covered *Over Easy* yet? At home?"

Bambi-brown eyes turned sharply assessing. "Now, why would you think that?"

"Rumor has it you ride on occasion."

"Seriously? People are still talking about that ride?"

"In mythical terms."

She snorted. "I haven't ridden *Eggs*."

"Has anyone?"

"Cowboy, no one's even come close. He takes extreme exception to being ridden, flank strap or no flank strap. He's the real deal."

"What's he like once the rider's on the ground?" An important question for any bull rider to ask.

"Not as bad as some. I can't say I like your chances if you're in his way but he doesn't usually go looking for trouble."

"And if a rider gets hung up?"

"Good question. I've not seen it yet. You're my guinea pig."

"Ro, you're not exactly filling me with confidence about riding left-handed." It had to be said.

"Don't take my advice, then. Do it your way."

Her studied nonchalance lit a fire in his belly. "No, I'll take your advice. Do you like steak and jacket potatoes? I like steak and jacket potatoes. I saw a steakhouse on the way in."

"Cockiness will get you hammered by this one, cowboy," she said as she walked away. "Enjoy your meal."

CASEY WHILED AWAY the rest of the afternoon, waiting with increasing impatience for the show to begin. It was always the same, the welcome patter accompanied by bright lights, loud rock music and flames burning into the sky. Spectators in the stands were looking to be entertained, no question, but there was also plenty of downtime between rides, and they used that time for eating and drinking and getting better acquainted with their neighbors.

It wasn't that the crowd was bored. It was more that there were no sporting teams or major rivalries involved. It was bull against man and there were long seconds of heart-in-mouth action during a ride. In between those moments, though, people looked for release.

Casey was riding second to last on account of going into the round in second place, and already there was a new leader on the scoreboard. He needed an eighty-seven-point ride to put him at the top of the board, and even then there'd be one more rider after him still capable of pulling off the win.

He could do this.

When Rowan stepped up beside him and reached for the flank rope, Casey turned to look at her. "You're flank man? Woman? Since when?" Wasn't often he saw her in this role.

"My breeding program, my bull," Rowan murmured. "And I know how and when to tie his flank strap. If you have any objections, take it up with management."

"No objections," he was quick to assure her. But she was going to have to lean over the rail a fair way when tying off, and more than one cowboy was going to be looking in her direction, and sexy competence was hellishly distracting. And then Paulo slipped into place and Casey turned his attention to matters more at hand, like lowering himself onto the bull's back and getting his rope where he wanted it and having Paulo hold it tight so Casey could run his hand up and down it and warm up the fresh rosin on his glove to make it stickier. Paulo never had much to say once they got down to business; he was all focused strength and competence. Didn't hurt to have that around you in the chute.

Paulo tightened the rope, and at Casey's nod, handed it over for the wrap.

Now Rowan was tightening the flank strap. The bull moved restlessly beneath him as Casey put his weight right up on his left hand and got into position, reaching into his vest pocket with his free hand for his mouth guard. No more prep. He had this.

Paulo pulled his hand away.

Eyes firmly fixed between the gray bull's shoulders, Casey nodded.

Harper's bull let him keep that confidence for a split second as he burst from the chute and came up for air.

Casey tried not to get too far back in the pocket, and even managed it for several more seconds, riding well, riding as planned, getting ready to rake with his leg.

And then that son of Satan changed direction on him in midair and he was too far back and listing the wrong way. On the next buck he saw daylight and it was all over bar the flying without wings.

He saw more air than the bull, landed hard, and didn't bounce back up.

The eight-second siren went off a short time later. Adrenaline got Casey on his feet and moving back toward the chute he'd come from. Someone handed him his rope and bells and he staggered as he took hold of them. Not a good sign. Someone opened the gate and let him in and shut the gate behind him, away from the hungry eyes of the crowd. Paulo was there to steady him.

Rowan was there too, leaning over the rail in duplicate or maybe triplicate. Six eyes in total.

Spiders had six eyes. Some of them.

"That was a good start," said Paulo. "And then there was that steaming pile of ugly at the end."

Casey agreed with him, but nodding only set him to swaying the other way this time.

"Whoa." Paulo again, as he ducked his head to get a better look at Casey's face. And then one of the sports medics who toured with them was shouldering Paulo out of the way and shining a flashlight in Casey's eyes.

"Concussion," Casey offered helpfully, and batted away the too-bright pen light. He'd ridden the way Ro told him to. Ridden his best and hadn't got hung up at the end but there was no way he'd won that bet. "Sorry, Ro. No steak for you. You're not a vegan, are you? Because, steak, Ro. And potatoes. Sour cream. Mushroom gravy … mmm … baby peas. Do you like baby peas, Ro?" He could order baby peas for her. In their pods. She could pick the pods up with her fingers and suck the peas out one by one. "That'd be hot."

"Romeo, tell us more." Paulo sounded hugely entertained, and Rowan's six eyes were rolling around a lot as the medic shuffled Casey out of the chute and headed them for the medical treatment room deep beneath the arena seating. Every arena had a designated area, and if it didn't they set up a tent. The medic, Ross? Ron? Ronross the medic let him lean against the wall once they were away from the crowd. Not that he left Casey alone, no. Instead he put a hand to Casey's shoulder and looked quite unlovingly into his eyes once more.

"Bad?" Casey rasped.

"Not too bad. The peas are a worry though."

Right. Probably no point trying to explain his line of thought there.

They laid him out on a stretcher once he reached the treatment room and Doc Freeman started in on him.

"How's your vision?"

"Blurred."

"How's the light?"

"Way too goddamn bright."

"How's the headache on a scale of one to ten, with ten the most painful?"

"Two."

"Course it is. That's why you can barely stand up," said the doc. "Want to try that one again?"

"Six." He'd had worse.

He thought he saw Rowan, hovering at the edge of the room. He thought he might have said something about food. Right before he rolled to the edge of the stretcher and promptly lost breakfast, morning tea and lunch.

Chapter Two

BULL RIDERS GOT concussed on a regular basis. It was an undisputable fact and Rowan had lived with that knowledge since before she was old enough to understand what concussion meant. Blunt force trauma to the head. Traumatic brain injury. Bruising. Bleeding. Just because you couldn't see it, didn't mean it wasn't happening.

Rowan far preferred broken bones and muscle tears.

She should have been helping load up, and she did her job the way she always did, but when it was time to get in the truck and begin the haul back to the overnight livestock facilities the tour had arranged, she looked her father in the eye and told him she wanted to stick around for the night.

"Why?" Her father was never one to mince words.

"I want to do some clothes shopping in the morning."

"You." One word, heavy on the disbelief, and, okay, it wasn't the brightest excuse she'd ever come up with.

"Well, yeah. I saw a dress in a shop window this morning and thought I might go in when the shop was open and try it on."

"You. In a dress."

"Maybe." She hunkered into herself, head down, and toed the dirt with her boot. No fancy cowboy boots for her, she wore plain leather, steel-capped work boots and didn't regret it. She didn't look up. She had her mother's eyes, her father had once told her in a fit of drunken rambling.

Right before telling her to get out of his sight.

Sometimes it was best not to look at him when his mood was uncertain. "Maybe I thought I could give it a try, yes." The last time she'd worn a dress she'd been eighteen, a bridesmaid for her cousin, and there had been apricot frills involved. "I'm thinking I might dial back on the frills this time."

"Good idea." She had no idea why her father's voice had softened so much between one comment and the next. Maybe he *wanted* her to embrace her feminine side. "Do you need money?"

"I have money, Dad." He paid her to work and she barely spent any of it.

"Here." A wad of notes appeared in front of her downturned face. "It's been a while since we had a forty-six bull score. When you get home we'd best look at working up a schedule that'll give that bull of yours a shot at Vegas."

"Really?" This time she did look up, brown eyes meeting the cornflower blue of her father's as her smile began to spread. She'd had to fight him every step of the way before he'd even let her *load* lightweight crossbred 'Eggs' *Over Easy* onto one of their trucks destined for an AEBR event. Her father in turn had had to convince the tour's livestock manager that *Over Easy* was a bull to watch.

So far, the gamble was working.

"I was wrong; you were right. Take it." The money was still there. "Don't come home without something you like. And I don't mean a new belt or set of spurs."

"I do have enough belts to last me a while," she offered. She'd been collecting them since she was a child, and—what was worse—many of them still fit. There was a downside to being five foot two and a hundred and six pounds dripping wet. "Thanks."

He fished a set of keys out of his pocket next. "Take the Chevy. And don't be spending the night around here. Get yourself a room somewhere nice."

"What is this, my birthday?" she asked as she swapped keys with him.

"I can spoil my daughter if I want to."

"You *are* in a good mood." And so he should be. Their old bull champion, *Road to Ruin*, had been ridden for the win today. *Road to Ruin*'s brother *Hammerfall* had pulled a forty-three. If anyone had won this event hands down it was Harper Bucking Bulls. "We might even have a shot at the bull team challenge in Cheyenne?" A hundred thousand dollars for the winning team of three bulls. And currently, Harper Bucking Bulls had three very good bulls on the road.

"We'll talk about that too."

Plenty to talk about, yes. She suspected one thing she

wouldn't be talking about was her quiet need to see Tomas James Casey get up off that medical stretcher. She nodded at nothing in particular and turned on her heel.

"Rowan?"

Her father's gruff voice stopped her in her tracks. He could probably smell the lie on her. Since when had she ever been interested in clothes?

"Don't you go partying with any of those cowboys tonight."

"You know I never do." That much was truth. "But I might ask after Casey before I leave. See if he's standing."

"You're not responsible for every cowboy who wrecks off the back of one of our bulls. It's their choice to ride. They don't want to do anything else."

"I know that, Dad. I just want to check on him. You know I don't like concussion injuries." She'd had one herself and a bad one at that. "See you in Montgomery."

She walked away fast, before her father could call her back to dispense even more advice. She knew the rules—she'd heard them often enough. No sleeping around, never more than two drinks, no dating AEBR officials and emphatically no dating bull riders. Those rules had been laid down shortly after her sixteenth birthday and hadn't changed since.

Where her father expected her to find a suitable date was anyone's guess.

She didn't know anyone or anything else but this life. And in the midnight darkness where secrets lived she would reluctantly admit she was tired of it.

Maybe tomorrow she *would* buy a dress.

CASEY GOT LET out of the sports medicine room two hours after the winner had been announced. The crowd had left but the lights were still on. Paulo had come in third, Casey an almost respectable fifth. It said a lot for the quality of the bulls that only four riders had managed to stick their rides in the final round. That or the riders simply weren't trying hard enough.

He had a grade two concussion, a referral for an MRI if symptoms persisted, and the only reason they let him go was because they were packing up equipment all around him and he'd told them he had a ride back to the hotel and didn't want to wait around for one of them to take him.

Doc Freeman had checked his eyes and ears, made him count fingers (one), made him walk in a straight line to the door and back, and then made him recite a bad Irish limerick before finally pronouncing him good to go. The doc had then doled out a truly stingy number of painkillers (two). Two more could be had tomorrow, so as to save everyone the hassle of Casey getting back to his hotel room tonight and taking all four at once and overdosing.

It had been done before, albeit not by him.

"Anyone staying with you tonight?" Doc Freeman had

asked.

"Not yet."

"Someone needs to wake you after you've been asleep for a couple of hours to ask you comprehension questions all over again."

"I know the drill." Which didn't sound very grateful. "Thanks."

"Any unusual symptoms through this next week, you get to a hospital."

"Will do, Mom."

"Don't you old woman me."

"Don't insult my mother. My mother's young."

"And recently widowed, or so I hear. Sorry to hear about your father."

Travis Freeman, the team doctor, was a good man. Casey nodded. He didn't want to talk about it. "Thanks again."

Head down he'd made his way along the long, narrow walkway toward the exit, not even seeing Rowan until he plowed into her. He steadied her, or she steadied him, he couldn't quite tell. He muttered an apology that might have been more heartfelt if the jolt hadn't felt as if someone had stabbed him in the eye with an ice pick.

"Sorry," he said again, and he should probably let go of her arm anytime now. God, she was tiny. Arms like kindling and, "Do you bruise?" He bet she bruised easily. He bet she'd have his fingerprints on her arm tomorrow. Horrified, he stepped back, straight into a cinder block wall.

"Whoa. Easy, cowboy. You right there?" She was steadying him *again*, had her hands on him *again*, and in his current state of not quite tracking well, having her hands on him *at all* was a little bit too much. It gave him ideas.

"Sorry," he mumbled again, and took a careful step away from her until he was standing on his own two feet without her support.

"You almost had him," she said next. Her voice was light but her eyes were doing a thorough job of assessing him, although he wasn't quite sure what for. "The bull."

"Wasn't long enough."

"Better than any other cowboy on that bull so far."

"Still not long enough."

"Oh, you're one of *those*." She fell back a little, gave him some room to move, which he did, toward the exit. And then she fell into step beside him. "Hard to be around when you don't cover your ride."

"Am not. I'm very easy to be around *all the time*." Could be he heard his brothers howling with laughter from afar. Could be he was still concussed.

"Are you heading back to the hotel?"

He risked another nod and regretted it immediately.

"Want me to drive you there?" she asked.

That could work. "You're heading past?"

"Yes," she said. "I've had a change of plans. I'm sticking around for a day or so. I want to buy a dress."

"I'd like to see that. Not the buying of a dress, but you in a dress. That I'd like to see. Pretty. But you're always pretty." It was the drugs. Or the concussion. Had to be. Why else would his mouth not stop running?

"Okay, cowboy." Now she was humoring him. "You traveling with anyone at the moment?"

"Just me." Which suited him fine, all things considered.

"Do you trust me to drive your truck?" she asked, and he blinked, because her dropping him off at the hotel was one thing, but her driving his truck there was something altogether different. "Remembering that I'm fully capable of hauling a stock carrier loaded with bulls," she said dryly. "I'm offering to drive you and your truck to the hotel and park you both there and then get a lift back to collect my ride."

"And you're staying where?"

"At the hotel."

"And why are you driving there twice?"

"Casey, do yourself a favor and stop trying to think. I'm doing you a favor."

"Why?"

"Because you took my advice and I can count on one finger the number of people who do that. I'm feeling generous toward you. Where's your truck?"

"Where's my gear?" His rope. His hat. He'd lost track of them.

Rowan sighed. "Paulo picked them up. He probably put them in your truck, assuming he knows what it looks like, which I don't. What are you driving?"

"A cherry red Chevy. 1967. Me'n'm'brothers restored it last winter. Runs like an angel, guzzles gas like the devil. Inconspicuous."

"You keep telling yourself that, buddy," she muttered beneath her breath, and slipped her hand through his elbow, and he smiled at her afresh and crooked his arm because now they were walking out from beneath the stadium seating together and that was what he wanted. "I can probably find your inconspicuous little Chevy fairly easily, even if you can't remember where you parked it. I'm offering to get you, your ride and your gear to the hotel. You planning on taking me up on it or are you going to be stubborn about it?"

"Taking you up on it," he said, and left off the nod because he was a smart, smart man.

People noticed her attention toward him as they made their way from the coliseum and the fair grounds—of course they did. Secrets were hard to keep when on tour. Didn't need to be a secret, the way Ro told it.

Not as if he was aiming to do wrong by her, no, sir.

Get the poor, concussed cowboy to his room, that's all.

She said it to people half a dozen times before they even reached his truck. "You're protesting too much about being seen with me," he offered helpfully. "It's your guilty conscience."

"I haven't done anything!"

"Yet."

He didn't think he was mistaking concern for attraction. Not with the way her breath caught as they both reached for the passenger door of his truck and their fingers tangled. Not with the way her gaze hitched on his mouth and stayed there. Not for the full eight seconds, no, but long enough.

"Like what you see?" he murmured, and she put her hand to his vest as if to push him away only she didn't push him away so much as stare at her hand and then snatch it away as if burnt. "It's hotter beneath the vest," he assured her. He needed core strength to stick his ride and his abs could rival anyone's. "Feel free to check."

"You're going to be so embarrassed later."

Probably not. He got into his truck, passenger side, and that was just plain wrong but he suffered in silence and she drove him to the hotel. He approved her gear changes with a measured hum.

Once inside she steered him toward the reception desk and got him to get a second room-card from reception because he couldn't find the first, and then she piled him into the elevator and took him to his room.

"I hate to break it to you, Ro, but we spoke to three more tour people on our way in and they know you don't usually stay at the tour hotel and you're still over-explaining your involvement with me. You sure you know what you're doing? Seeing as you're not intending to go out with me an' all?"

"I have a plan," she said as she opened the door to his

room and pushed him inside. "It involves putting you solidly in the friend zone for all to see. Nothing else happening here."

"Oh, that's harsh." Not to mention wrong. Because there was plenty happening here. "Why don't you want anyone to know?"

"Know what?"

"Know what you want."

Silence, thick and uncomfortable.

"You are allowed to go after what you want," he murmured.

"Your ego's as big as the sun," she told him.

"Not quite." Healthy though, and he saw no reason to deny it. He'd been blessed with a hard body, a face women sighed over and a brain in there somewhere. "Wasn't actually talking about me."

Silence again.

"Tell me about the dress you want," he said, more for conversation and getting rid of the awkward silence than any great interest in clothing. "What color is it?"

"I haven't bought it yet." She sounded a little cross. He started to reach for the buckle on his chaps and then thought better of it. Perhaps he should hold off on the undressing until after she left.

"It could be cherry red like my truck."

"We all have our little fantasies. You planning to get any of your riding gear off anytime soon?"

"No, ma'am." Because he'd stopped all that. Hadn't been thinking about getting him naked and her naked and them both beneath the shower *at all*.

"Sit down, cowboy. Let me at least help you get at your boots and your spurs. If you bend over to do it you're either going to pass out or throw up."

"Doubt it." There was nothing left to heave. But he sat on the bed and unbuckled his chaps—wasn't as if he didn't have jeans on beneath—and she helped him lose them and tugged his boots off while he unhitched his riding vest, and now he had even *more* fantasies to consider. "Why are you doing this again?"

She sat back on her haunches and looked up at him, her smile wry and her eyes serious. "I saw a cowboy ride once, get knocked out, get up five minutes later, act a little confused for a couple of hours after that and then die later that night in his sleep. Or not in his sleep. Hard to say because no one was there with him when they should have been."

"Someone you knew well?"

"Not that well, but it left a mark on everyone around at the time. Not to mention that I told you how to ride and I might be feeling a little guilty about the end result."

"Nothing for you to feel guilty about. That's just stupid."

Her eyes narrowed.

"Not that I'm calling you stupid. No sirree. What I mean to say is that you're not responsible for my inability to cover my ride. Or for what happens afterward."

"I'm going to look in on you later, okay?" she said, standing up and pocketing his swipe card.

"I knew you wouldn't be able to resist me for long."

"You keep telling yourself that and I'll keep wallowing in my guilt, and I'm *still* going to look in on you later."

"Do you like peas?" he asked, and made her blink.

"I do."

"I knew it," he said. And then she left and he sagged back onto the bed, and closed his eyes and then nothing.

Cowboys were big gossips, Rowan decided several hours later as she closed her tab and said her goodbyes and made sure everyone saw her leave alone. Her father had wanted her to stay somewhere other than the official tour hotel, but she didn't *have* to take his advice. The tour hotels were four star, minimum, and she liked the reassurance of being surrounded by familiar faces.

She'd already made Doc Freeman go up and check on Casey once—by the simple act of mentioning that Casey had been more than a little out of it on the trip back to the hotel. Not quite watching his words the way he usually would.

That was when Doc Freeman had mentioned that Casey's father had died just before Vegas last year and had been buried the weekend of the finals. Rowan had sat back in silence as everything about Casey's absence late last year came crashing into place.

Family first, he'd said. Family before buckles and winnings, confetti and a possible million-dollar paycheck with his name on it.

His father dead.

Why the hell hadn't he *said* anything, the close-mouthed bastard?

IT ONLY MADE sense for Rowan to check on Casey later that evening. She'd said she would, Doc Freeman's efforts notwithstanding. She was on the same floor as him, a few doors down, and if no one was in the corridor to see her all the better. She rapped lightly on his door, and when that got no response, let herself into his room with the key she'd pocketed earlier.

Casey had obviously showered at some point and forgotten to put half his clothes back on. Instead of jeans he wore soft-looking black sweats that showcased his perfectly rounded ass, and although he'd managed to push bedcovers aside, he definitely hadn't opted to pull them back over him. It left his back and arms bare and glowing golden in the lamplight, and Rowan looked her fill at muscles honed for fast-twitch responses rather than endurance. She could smell eucalyptus body wash and beneath it the tantalizing scent of man, warm and clean, and something about it made her blood thicken and slow, the better to absorb the scent.

She'd been hoping Casey would wake as she came in so that she'd feel less like an intruder—or a voyeur—but it hadn't happened yet and his body had that boneless quality of someone deeply asleep.

Or possibly unconscious.

"Hey, cowboy." She edged a little closer and tried not to stare. He had one arm beneath his pillow and the other outstretched beside him, and don't let her get started on the corded musculature in his arms. Not too built, not too underdeveloped, and too damn perfect. "Casey."

Nothing.

"Tomas James. T.J." The man had a lot of names. She pushed lightly at his shoulder and tried to ignore the silky warmth of his skin beneath her fingertips. "Hey lover. Stud." He wasn't answering to those either. "Big boy?" Hard to tell given that he was lying on his stomach, but a woman could hope. "Ready for round two?"

Casey groaned and cracked open the eye that wasn't currently smooshed into the pillow.

"Atta boy. Now tell me your name."

"You know my name."

True. "But do you?"

"Tomas James Casey."

Sweet. She felt like a schoolmarm taking roll call. "And what day is it?"

"Sunday, unless it's gone midnight," he murmured. "Which it might have."

"Not yet. How old are you?"

"Thirty-one."

"And how many serious relationships have you had?"

He rolled over onto his back and there was one question answered at any rate. Tomas James Casey was packing *plenty* of weight in the big boy department.

"Why? See something you like?" he murmured and she tore her gaze from his low-slung sweats and stuck her hand in her jeans pocket for the little bottle of over-the-counter pain meds she'd picked up. She sat the bottle beside the water on the bedside table instead.

"I got you these," she said.

"Thank you. You still fixing to go dress shopping in the morning?"

Nothing wrong with his memory. "Yeah." She risked a glance toward his face, and if she needed any more proof that his concussion wasn't all that severe, there it was. His eyes were clear, nothing hazy or unfocused about them, and they really were the most unusual deep forest green. No flecks of gold, no hazel, no blue. Just green and darker green, softening to gray around the edges. "Just checking up on you. I'll go now."

"Stay."

Bad idea. "No can do, cowboy. Far be it for me to take advantage of the sick and the poor."

"M'not either. Going back to college soon."

"To do what?" She had no idea who he was beyond bull riding, but she'd pegged him for a rancher's son.

"Vet."

"You've started?"

"Finished my undergrad. Did my first year of postgrad. Ran out of money and started riding bulls. That was five years ago."

"Do you even *like* riding bulls?" She'd never considered that this wasn't his first choice when it came to what he wanted to do with his life.

"I like it well enough when it pays," he said with a tired smile. "What do you do when you're not hauling stock?"

"I breed bucking bulls," she said as he raised his arms to the headboard and stretched, and, oh. He didn't *just* have a six-pack. He had an entire continent of hills and valleys and ridges just waiting to be explored.

"Ever wanted to do anything else?" he murmured.

She was rapidly coming to the conclusion that she wanted to do *him*, but that was a conclusion better left unsaid.

"Sometimes I do. But it's the family business, you know? And I don't know anything else." She'd been homeschooled on the road and while she thought she was okay education wise, rocking up to college had never been on her agenda. "I take photos sometimes—some of those have made it into bull-riding tour brochures and magazines—but the subject matter is right there, and I'm there too, most of the time, so if the light's right I'll get the camera out. It's mostly behind the scenes stuff. People packing up when the glitz and glamor show is over."

"Do you take photos of anything else?"

"Ranch life. Wildlife. Wyoming." She'd read his publicity bio. She read them all. She didn't usually memorize them all, and also, some of those bios were more fiction than fact. "You're from Montana, right?"

"Yeah. My family's been ranching there since the early nineteen hundreds. It's a good spread but it doesn't sustain five sons. I'm second youngest and I need another way to earn a living. Something helpful when it comes to the family business but portable too, you know?"

She nodded as if she did know what it was like to contemplate going her own way, but the truth was she never had. She was her father's only living child, although not the son he'd always wanted. She was fully involved in the family business. She had her own bull breeding program—*Over Easy* was part of it. She owned half the ranch outright—her mother's half—not that she ever advertised that fact. She had resources that took generations to build and opportunities others envied. It wasn't a *bad* life.

She'd lost count of the cowboys trying to get into her pants so as to claim a piece of it.

"Where will you go when you start studying again?" she asked.

"Not sure yet. Washington State or UC Davis. Depends

how much money I make this year. The more money the better my options."

"And then what?"

"And then I don't know."

"But not back to bull riding?"

"C'mon, Ro. You know as well as me this is no sport for old men. Gotta have an exit plan."

She nodded again, frowning. "A lot of cowboys look at me and see one." There. She'd said it.

He sat up suddenly, and swung his legs over the edge of the bed. "Is that what you think I'm doing?"

"Probably." In all honesty. "Yes."

He really was too pretty for his own good. Messy dark hair, strong jaw, great lips and a fair bit of shadow defining them. Expressive eyes that seemed to telegraph his every emotion—and how he'd survived *that* trait with four brothers was anyone's guess.

His current emotion was pissed off.

Just a guess.

"How about I say that if I married into a wealthy family—like yours—I'd still not want to work for either you or your father? I'd rather keep my balls. But there's the door if you don't believe me." He nodded toward it.

"I was going anyway." She put the hotel door card on the bedside table and headed for the door, only by the time she went to open it he was right there beside her, his hand on the handle as he opened it for her. He was so close she could see the flawlessness of his skin and the unearthly length of his lashes.

"I still want that dinner," he rumbled. "I'd still like nothing more than to see what kind of sense we make, in bed and out, but not for the reasons you think. I like you, Rowan. I like the way you look and the way you move, the way you work, and the way you make my body ache in all the right places. I'd like to know more." He pulled the door wide open and stood aside to let her leave. "I'm drawn to *you*. Not your money or your father's bulls. Is that so hard to believe?"

"It's a little unexpected."

"Try looking in the mirror some time."

"I do."

He said nothing to that, just stood there, eyeing her steadily, as if he could see every insecurity she'd ever owned.

"Thanks for checking on me," he said finally.

She nodded jerkily, shoved her hands in the pockets of her baggy jeans and wished she hadn't left her cap in her room. She could have hidden her confusion beneath it.

Her room was on the twelfth floor, same as his. She'd asked for one here, but as he watched her walk the three doors and fish her card from her pocket, she wondered if that too hadn't been a bad idea in a day full of them.

He was still watching, leaning against his doorframe as she pushed her way inside her room and let the door thud closed behind her.

So the man had ambitions beyond the world she'd been

born to. That was good, right? He wasn't a fortune hunter out to charm his way into Harper Bucking Bulls. He wasn't a cowboy bent on riding bulls until his body gave out. He was here for what he could rightfully earn and once he earned enough to see him through his studies he'd be gone. He'd meet a college girl with golden hair and a sunny smile and she'd be studying law or medicine and hosting dinner parties on the side.

What would he want with a woman whose main claim to education consisted of knowing every back road and cheap gas station between Wyoming and Texas?

What was she even doing here, hovering around him like some fool?

She let her head thud against the back of the door and jumped when someone knocked back in reply. The knock sounded again, so she opened the door cautiously.

Casey.

"I forgot to thank you for the riding advice," he said, and leaned forward, snaked his hand around her neck and kissed her.

It really wasn't a *thank you* kiss. It was an *I'm starving and you're so damn tasty* kiss. One that started hot and slid straight into downright filthy between one second and the next. A kiss that promised absolute abandon and no regrets and her hand went to his chest and her fingers curled and that moan of approval … She was pretty sure it was hers.

She tilted her head to allow him better access and boy

did he take it. Man wasn't slow when it came to gathering her close and letting her know by the hardness of his body and the heat in his touch that he hadn't been lying when he'd said he wanted her.

Maybe even *just* her.

She craved one last kiss and took it before putting her hand to his abdomen and pushing him away. "You don't have to thank me for riding advice." She was breathless and too soft-voiced for her own good but at least she wasn't begging him to take her to bed and love her forever.

"Let me take you to breakfast," he rasped.

"Not a good idea." People would see and draw their own conclusions.

"Do it anyway." Gravel-rough and so compelling, he had a voice that stroked her senses. "What time do you eat?"

"Six."

He groaned, and now *there* was a sound that would keep her company tonight. "Have a heart, Ro. I'm walking wounded."

"And you call yourself a cowboy."

"Bull rider. Special breed. Worthy of respect."

"Uh-huh." It wasn't easy to sound bored in the presence of T.J. Casey's bare chest but she did her best.

"Respect and the occasional concession when it comes to five a.m. awakenings."

"I might have breakfast at eight," she said. She had no real reason beyond habit to get up at five tomorrow morning. She could sleep in. Daydream a little. Probably about him.

"I'll be downstairs in the breakfast room at eight. You won't regret it," he said.

She already did.

"Sweet dreams, Rowan."

Close the door; don't call him back. Don't start something you can't finish. Those were the thoughts that swirled and meshed with the memory of his kiss. Be a grown-up. Have breakfast. State very plainly that nothing could come of his interest, never mind the pull she felt toward him. She couldn't afford to screw around on tour and get a reputation—not when tour management barely tolerated her presence in the first place. As for his career, there were a hundred and one subtle ways her father and his ilk could make Casey pay if he didn't treat her right.

Rowan was simultaneously unwanted and overprotected by those around her.

Story of her life.

Chapter Three

CASEY WOKE WITH the mother of all headaches and a body that knew it had gone seven seconds with a sixteen-hundred-pound bull yesterday and lost. It took a ten-minute shower, as hot as he could stand it, two painkillers and a shot of caffeine before he even began to feel human again. He packed his duffel and hauled it out to his truck before heading back to the hotel's breakfast area. He'd coerced Rowan Harper into having breakfast with him this morning—he remembered that much, and the kiss that went with it. But it was already five after eight and it'd serve him right if she didn't turn up.

She was sitting in the breakfast area, at a table for four—that was the good news. But she wasn't alone.

Flynn Davis, who toured the circuit as one of the rodeo clowns, sat at the table too, and so did Gisele, one of the new bull-rider wives on the tour. Gisele had come from old money back East and stood out like a prickle on a pumpkin on the tour. Casey looked for her husband, Kit, but he was nowhere to be seen.

"I saved you a seat," said Rowan as he approached, and

he blinked, because that sounded … intimate.

"I told him I'd see him at breakfast so I'd know he didn't die in his sleep," she told the other two, and there was the save. Nothing to see here.

"It was only a little concussion," he protested.

"That's what they all say," Ro muttered darkly. "And the next minute they're dead."

"Aren't you a ray of sunshine in the morning. More coffee, anyone?"

"Not for me. I'm about to take my leave but thank you, Casey," said Gisele. Manners of a queen, that one, and an accent to match, but she never looked down on anyone and often sought Rowan's company. Casey nodded and looked to Flynn.

"Gonna get one to go," said the other man. "The road calls."

"Black," said Rowan. "Thanks."

By the time he returned with two coffees only Rowan remained, and wasn't that a convenient way to ease into having breakfast with this woman? They hadn't arrived together; they were just people who knew each other, seeking out a familiar face in a hotel breakfast room. Nothing to gossip about here, unless it was to do with Rowan staying on after her father had loaded up all the Harper bulls and left. Just a breakfast between colleagues.

Why this immediately made him want to lean over and claim her with a kiss was anyone's guess.

"Four brothers and I still hate sharing," he muttered instead, and made her smile. "What? It's the ugly truth. Not that we ever fought over a woman. Well, not to my knowledge."

"Did your mother ever long for a girl?"

"Of course. It's human nature to long for what you don't have."

Too late he remembered the story Paulo had told him about the Harper family tragedy. "Which would you prefer?" he asked. "Girl or boy?"

"Boy."

"Why so certain?"

"Because in my family setup, being male is an advantage. Rough stock contracting, bull riding—they're male domains."

"You manage."

"I'm tolerated. There's a difference."

"What if you had a son and he wanted to play football or become an accountant?"

"I guess the accounting would come in handy," she deadpanned. "Not sure about the football. Hard to commit to a team sport when you're on the road for most of the year."

"Good thing you're not a boy who likes football."

"Yes, but I did want to be a ballerina at one point. That's not even a sport. It's art."

"Right."

"Have you ever tried to pirouette your way through the snow while wearing snow boots and supposedly shoveling a path from the house to the barn?"

"No."

"Don't."

He liked this woman and the pictures she drew for him, never mind that she hadn't given him a straight answer when it came to children being encouraged to do their own thing. Or maybe she had given him a very clear answer on that. Any child of hers would be expected to hold the family line.

Now there was a point of difference between them.

"Have you eaten?" he asked.

"Not yet. I slept in. And then I had to dress up to go dress shopping."

The only difference between today's outfit and yesterday's was that she'd ditched the checked flannel overshirt. Her T-shirt was gray and her jeans were the kind of faded that city people paid a premium for. She wore no makeup. She carried no handbag. If he quizzed her, he figured she'd have a wallet or a money clip stashed in a pocket somewhere. "Ready to go buy the perfect outfit?"

She grimaced. "Can't wait."

"You should never go dress shopping alone, you know?"

"How do you know?" she asked, which … good point.

"I have girl cousins. I hear talk. And I'm willing to spend the morning helping you out. You helped me out yesterday with my ride—it seems only fair."

"I am not buying a cherry red dress to match your truck."

"I'll have you know I'm doing my very best to let go of that particular fantasy," he protested. "It's an excellent one, by the way. I revisited it again last night, after our kiss."

"Weren't you supposed to be sleeping last night? Doctor's orders?"

"I did that too." But he'd woken with a skull-cracker of a headache and had been up twice throughout the night checking his eyes in the mirror for blown pupils. There was a difference between being bred tough and being born stupid, and he liked to think he wasn't the latter. The last thing his family needed was another family member dead after a fall they hadn't taken seriously enough.

"I don't understand your desire to watch me buy clothing," she said with a frown crease between her eyes. "Do you expect me to make a fool of myself? Is it something to tease me about? Do you think I'm going to look all wrong?"

"Do *you*?"

She shrugged and dropped her gaze. "I'm not exactly known for my femininity."

"The work you do doesn't define you, Rowan. People only have to look beneath your ball caps and big sunglasses to know you could be breathtakingly feminine if you wanted to be. The foundation's there. You just have to want to go there—either for someone else or for yourself."

She nodded, but still wouldn't look at him.

"And I don't have to go shopping with you—don't mind me. I'm aware some journeys are more personal than others. And now I'm going to go raid the breakfast buffet for bacon and pancakes and more syrup than I deserve. May I get you some?"

"Look at you with the manners and the thoughtfulness." She was smiling again and that was how he wanted her. "Who'd have guessed?"

"Exactly," he said agreeably. "Although my mother might have guessed. She spent enough time drilling manners into us when we were kids. Not a lot of use for them on the back of a bucking bull, but I remember them well enough when I'm out of the arena and not halfway concussed. Do I need to apologize for last night?"

"Apologize for what?"

"Pushing too hard, declarations of intent, inappropriate kisses …" He watched color steal into her cheeks and figured he might not have to apologize for those kisses after all. "Possibly other things."

And then her chin came up and her gaze met his. "No need to apologize."

Well, all right then.

Rowan headed for the buffet and Casey followed, traveling his own path once they got there, filling his plate with proteins and fruit and going easy on the carbs. His exercise and nutrition plan wasn't as rigorous as Jett's when it came to muscle development and weight gain or loss, but he still had one, and he'd pit his core strength and balance against his brother's any day.

Rowan had a robust appetite for someone so small. She ate fast and didn't make small talk, looking up when she was done to find him only half-finished. And he'd been trying to keep apace with her.

"Shit," she said as hot color stole across her cheeks. She picked up her still-folded napkin and wiped her mouth and hands and then tucked her hands beneath her legs and looked away and colored some more.

It occurred to him that she'd never had a mother like his, one who'd been in full command of the riot at the dining table, telling them to slow down and keep their elbows to themselves, drumming the appropriate use of silverware into them whether they wanted to learn about cutlery choices or not.

He put his knife and fork together on the plate—some teachings could never be forgotten—and stood up. "Ready to shop?"

Because he was done making this woman feel uncomfortable.

She was more skittish away from the bulls, less confident, more vulnerable, and it called to every protective instinct he owned. If she wasn't careful she'd bite straight through her bottom lip and that would be a shame.

"Ready," she muttered, looking for all the world as if she was headed straight for the gallows.

"Want me to come?"

Rowan shrugged. "I've no idea where to look or what kind of clothes I want, which suggests it might take forever, but you could come along and give your opinion if you want."

"I want."

TWENTY MINUTES LATER they stood at the corner of a downtown high street that looked promising when it came to boutiques full of women's clothes. There was the western store on the corner that seemed to specialize in fancy cowboy boots and men's clothes too, as well as women's clothes both casual and fancy. There was the boutique that specialized in making businesswomen look businesslike. There was a shop for jeans, a shop for tops, a shop for teens and a bar and grill. Rowan could park him here and come back when she was done and he wouldn't complain, but that wasn't what he'd signed on for so he dutifully followed her inside the boutique that caught her eye.

It was one of those stores where the colors of the clothes were all muted grays and tans, liberally sprinkled with white linen jackets and the occasional skirt or elegant black cocktail dress. The shop assistant was a tall, blonde woman in her fifties and she stared at Rowan curiously.

"May I help you?" she asked.

"Yes, I'm looking for a dress. For me," Rowan said with a nervous smile.

"What sort of dress?"

"Ah—"

"Something formal? Evening wear?"

"No."

The woman tried again. "A day dress to wear to a meeting? A sundress to feel pretty in?"

"The last one," said Rowan.

The woman nodded and cast a quick glance at Casey. "Here's what I'm going to do. I'm going to save you the trouble of trying anything on that's in this shop and tell you outright that my clothes are not going to suit you—and that's not an insult. You're too petite and these clothes are built for tall women with plenty of curves and confidence. In other words, my clothes are going to swim on you. Moreover, they're designed for a … shall we say more mature clientele? Like me. May I ask what lured you in here?"

"The blue of that dress." Rowan gestured toward it and the woman nodded.

"It's a beautiful gray-blue, a favorite of mine too, but it's going to do nothing for you."

"Oh."

Stripped of what little confidence she'd started with; that was what Rowan was in that moment. Casey saw it but didn't know how to fix it. The saleswoman woman saw it too.

"Try the blue frock on, by all means. Try anything you want on in here and I'll help you make the best of it," the saleswoman continued with utter confidence. "But if you don't mind taking my advice and spending a bit of money, I'll tell you to make a beeline for the western boutique on the corner instead. Ignore the brightly colored embroidered pieces, forget the suede, and head for the back of the shop behind the boots section. You'll find a collection of crushed chiffon sundresses with spaghetti straps and fitted bodices. The dresses will fall probably to your knees and you might want to take the hem up, but the rest should work for you. Now, they don't have them in blue, but they do have one in cream with caramel accents and that's the one for you. Dress size zero to two—that's your size, in case you didn't know. Pair it with deep-red fancy boots and then and *only* then take a look in the mirror. Tell them Nancy sent you."

This time it was Casey who nodded as he opened the door and held it for Ro. "Thank you, ma'am."

"Yes. I—thank you."

"My pleasure." The woman held the door open for them both. "You're going to look beautiful."

IF ROWAN HADN'T been so embarrassed she might have made a better show of thanking the woman. As it was, only Casey's presence stopped her from fleeing the shopping strip altogether and heading for the nearest wide-open space.

"She seemed nice." Casey looked at Rowan from beneath his cowboy hat. "Although it could be she typecast you because of my hat. Do you *want* western clothes?"

She had no idea.

"Because you don't *have* to follow her suggestion. I can see you in Audrey Hepburn clothes too."

"You're a movie buff?"

"Blame my mother. She used to iron to *Breakfast At Tiffany's*. You've got that same look about you as Audrey Hepburn had. Pure thoroughbred."

Rowan blinked. "You can't be serious."

"Maybe not the tiara," he offered casually, and then they were at the door of the western store and those doors slid open all by themselves.

Inside was more like a department store than she expected—a department store with a western slant. They found the boots easily enough. Women's to the left and the men's boots on the right. Casey found the men's belt racks. Rowan found the dresses, and they were far more ethereal than the woman had described and more expensive than Rowan could have imagined. Beautiful though, and she rubbed the silky material between her thumb and fingertips. So soft and almost sheer, and the tag said 100% pure silk, which might explain the price.

Casey, meanwhile, had attracted the attention of not one but two of the female shop attendants.

Figured.

She found her size and caught the eye of an older woman in the menswear section. Rowan took the dress from the rack and gestured with it toward the nearby change rooms. The woman nodded in assent but otherwise made no fuss of her.

Maybe this *was* her kind of place after all. In and out fast, no spotlight. Dress purchased.

She was standing there in panties, with the dress halfway over her head when a youthful voice came at her from the other side of the curtain.

"Ma'am, this is Wendy. The cowboy with the eyes to die for asked me to find out your shoe size."

Eyes to die for. There was no denying that particular description. Rowan didn't even begin to try.

"Size six," she said from beneath the layers of material.

Guess Casey had been paying more attention to the other woman's words than she had.

"How's the dress size?"

"Okay. I think. I haven't actually got it on yet."

"I'll be back in a little while. Take your time."

You too, Rowan wanted to say, but she tugged the dress over her head instead, and shimmied into the surprisingly snug bodice. Oh, so that was why there was no need for a bra with this dress. It had built-in support beneath the silk that lifted things and made things seem bigger than they were.

Fine by her.

"Ma'am? Wendy again. Try these boots with the dress."

The bottom left-hand corner of the curtain twitched and moments later a hand appeared, with a pair of red cowboy boots with fancy tan stitching. "Stocking socks are in the left boot," Wendy said. "And I've a very nice two-tone tan boot here, with red and orange stitching. You want to see them too?"

"Sure."

A second set of boots appeared beside the first. "There's a mirror out here when you're ready."

There was a mirror inside the cubicle too. Granted, it wasn't large but she could make do.

She reached for the red boots first and then hesitated. The tan ones were nicer and the toe was neatly rounded. The heel was a little higher too.

Couldn't hurt to try them on first.

And then she couldn't see everything in the mirror after all, so after a quick check for people, Rowan slipped from the dressing room and stood in front of the other mirror.

Shoulders that hadn't seen sunlight for years glowed pale and creamy beneath the trick lighting of the store, but there was no denying that the dress suited her, bringing out the deep brown of her hair and the whiskey color of her eyes. The boots gave her more height and the fabric seemed to fall right no matter which way she turned. She even had breasts, thanks to the magic bodice and the extra layers of fabric there.

And then Casey and one of the young shop attendants

appeared, and—in for a dollar, in for a thousand-dollar spend, what with the boots—but the outfit was feminine and pretty and not entirely uncomfortable. "What do you think?" she asked.

"I think the woman in the other shop knew what she was talking about," Casey said in a voice that sounded a little gruffer than it had at breakfast.

"Here," said the girl, Wendy, and handed her a long silver chain, with delicate links that were bigger than normal. A silver heart dangled from the center of it and it was too long and came almost to her belly button, but Casey smiled when she put it on, and there was that look again, the one that warmed her all over.

"Let me show you a trick with this one," said Wendy, and shuffled them both back into the change room and shut the curtain behind them. "You need to take the hem up but do this for now. You do the front; I'll do the back." And she turned Rowan around and very gently began to tuck some of the flowy part of the dress up beneath the bodice. "Two inches ought to do it."

Two inches later and Rowan stood in front of the mirror once more. The dress was coming home with her—that was a given. And so were the boots. And the necklace, which would undoubtedly find its way to the back of a drawer, never to be seen again. "I'll take it all."

"We have a top in this fabric too. Put your jeans on and the red boots and I'll bring it in."

The top was pale gold with cap sleeves and a modest V neck. It too was a little long in the bodice and she resigned herself to taking off another two inches all around.

The red boots were gorgeous, and there went another seven hundred dollars, just like that.

Casey was over at the counter, doubtless being chatted up, and then his gaze met hers, and he smiled slow and sure as he took in her outfit and gave it a nod.

Beside her, Wendy sighed. "He looks familiar."

"Pro bull rider."

"That'll do it," said Wendy with an even happier sigh. "Is he any good?"

"Better than good, but don't tell him I said so. It'll go to his head. I'll take the top and the red boots as well, and please don't show me anything else or my credit card will have a fit."

"Are you sure? The other outfit's already paid for. I say go for it. One more necklace. I know just the one. It's a bit of cord with a ceramic cross on it in red and bronze. You can hang on to it and pray when you watch your guy ride."

"He's not—"

Her guy.

And she was going to have to find a way to give back the money he'd spent on her. He needed it for his study fund. She fished out her credit card from her pocket. "Put these on this card. Put them *all* on this card but don't let him know."

"These ones I can put on your card," said the ever helpful Wendy. "But your cowboy there paid in cash, and for what it's worth, he didn't even flinch."

Shit. Rowan slipped out of the boots and the top and Wendy whisked them away. By the time Rowan got to the counter Casey had wandered off again to look at some hats and Wendy had found the necklace with the cross and it was every bit as pretty as promised.

Rowan left the shop laden with bags, more than a little giddy at finding clothes and accessories that looked good and made her feel just right. Girl clothes, yes. Softly feminine and pretty.

"Not that I've ever been dress shopping with a woman before but that was pretty quick and relatively painless," Casey said. "Are you happy with your purchases?"

"Yes. Less happy with you paying for some of it."

"I had to in case you decided not to buy them. You would have regretted it. Worse, I would have regretted it. I have a new bet," he said. "If I cover *Eggs For Breakfast* you have dinner with me while wearing those boots and that dress."

"They don't match your Chevy."

"Oh, but they do," he muttered with no little reverence. "I had a vision in the shop of exactly that."

"You have a very rich inner life," she said, and Casey grinned.

"No, I have eyes. Where to next? More shopping?"

"I doubt I could cope. You've already spent half your

weekend's winnings on me."

"True, I wasn't exactly in the money this weekend. I'll try harder next time."

He gave every ride his all, no matter what. It was why people paid to watch him ride. Why people would get behind him all over again and want him to go all the way and win the championship buckle. Also, he was so goddamn gorgeous at interview. The camera ate him up and he could string two words together and he never trash-talked anyone else. Poster boy for the sport—right up until the end of last year when he'd bailed and neglected to tell anyone that family tragedy was the reason for it.

"You realize I need to pay you back for the dress and the boots."

"No you don't. It was my pleasure."

But she refused to be beholden to him for this. It wasn't right. It wasn't her. "Will I see you in Atlanta? I'll fix you up there."

He nodded. "I'll be there. I'll be there to win."

Chapter Four

CASEY LIKED BEING in Atlanta. The lazy drawl and easy manners reminded him of his mother and her family, and the arena was an indoor one with corporate booths and club seats, high-end acoustics and concert-hall lighting and audio options. The sound and lighting guys invariably went mad with all the extra toys on offer and the crowd liked it. The more experienced bulls and cowboys put up with it.

He covered his first two rides and was sitting in fourth place going into the short go, but he hadn't drawn a Harper bull and didn't like his chances of pulling off a high-scoring ride with the bull he had drawn.

Rowan Harper was ignoring him. Every time he so much as looked at her she put her head down and disappeared. Even Paulo noticed.

"You asked her out, didn't you?" Paulo said as they sat waiting for Paulo's bull to come into the chute.

Like Casey, Paulo had made it through to the short go. Unlike Casey, Paulo had drawn a bull that actually had the potential to deliver him a winning ride.

"I did ask her out."

"I heard she stayed on and that you two ended up having breakfast together."

"That was all it was. There was no going out the night before. Rowan was having breakfast in the hotel dining room with Gisele and Flynn and I happened along."

"So you took advantage and sat on down."

"I sat down with all three of them, and then the other two left. Wasn't a date."

"You do realize her daddy's watching you watch her."

Casey smiled tightly and turned his head to meet Papa Harper's narrow gaze. "I'm aware." He held the older man's gaze a little too long for it to be mistaken for anything other than outright challenge. "He keeps her on too tight a leash. Doesn't have to be me who meets his approval but he can't deny his daughter the right to a life beyond that of a ranch hand. The sooner he realizes it the better for everyone."

Now Paulo was looking at him in flat appraisal, before shaking his head slightly and then turning it into a series of neck and shoulder stretches.

"C'mon. Here comes your bull," Casey said. "Time to get set."

"I hate coming out of the chute closest to the wall," Paulo muttered. "Every bad ride I've ever seen at this arena has come out of this chute."

"Don't be superstitious."

"It's not superstition if it's true." But Paulo was climbing over the rail and into the chute and time for talk was over.

Paulo never fussed once he sat a bull. He positioned his legs and set his rope, every movement swift and economical. He never riled the animal unnecessarily, never pumped himself up like some did. The man was a study in quiet, concentrated focus.

Paulo used a Brazilian bull rope, which meant he set his right hand well to the right of the bull's backbone. Different setup to the American bull rope Casey used, but equally effective. It was what you grew up with, what you got used to. When Paulo bumped his fist against the rope to signal it was as tight as he wanted it, Casey handed it over for the wrap and patted the other man on the chest. "Screw superstition. You've got this."

He honestly didn't care if it looked good or not that he still stood Paulo's bulls when he could or that Paulo was now sponsored by the same big-name sponsor who'd dumped Casey at the end of last season. He and Paulo were both riding well and sponsors counted for nothing during the seconds when it was just man and bull. The people you wanted at your side before those seconds started should damn well be the ones you trusted and wanted there.

The bull moved restlessly but Casey kept his hand pressed front and center to Paulo's vest. The kid acting as flank man, and he *was* a kid, was still fussing with the flank strap, and no sooner had he tightened it than the bull tried to climb its way out of the chute, rearing back, getting its feet up where they should never go and thrashing about as if possessed.

Sometimes a bull would settle but this one kept on fighting and with a curse Paulo released his rope hold and let Casey pull him off and out of harm's way. No rider liked a reset, and who the hell owned this bull and why weren't they releasing the flank strap and getting the animal settled?

But then Joe Harper was there, his hands sure and his movements calm as he leaned across the rail and loosened the flank strap back off.

"Show you a trick," he said to the boy who'd been acting as flank man, and then he looked toward Casey and Paulo as if to say what are you waiting for, and Paulo needed no second invitation to settle once more on the bull's back and trust Joe Harper to do absolutely right by him.

"No rider's going to wait for an engraved invitation the second time around. He knows full well we've already wasted enough of the bull's energy." Joe Harper's voice came low and reassuring as Paulo reset. Mouth guard already in, no time to waste as Casey tightened the rope again and held it taut as Paulo warmed up the rosin on his glove.

"This animal's going to bunch up the minute he feels that flank strap tighten so you want to wait as long as you can before disrupting the rider's preparation. Wait until you see the rider take his rope and start to wrap. That's your signal." Joe Harper was still talking, making it sound easy as he quietly called the shots. "See how Casey's got one hand on the rider's chest and one eye on us? We do our job and step back, Casey takes his hand away, the rider gives the nod and the gate opens. It's all in the timing. That's how we want this to go."

And that's how it went.

God damn the Brazilian could ride.

Eight seconds and eighty-five points later, Paulo sat at the top of the scoreboard.

Paulo resumed his position alongside Casey, eyes bright, doubtless pumped, as they watched the other riders roll through. None matched him although several came close.

Close wasn't good enough.

It was Casey's turn to ride in the next set. He caught Rowan's eye, right before the nod, and she smiled and suddenly the world was all right.

He stuck his ride and came off clean and uninjured. It was a good ride and the crowd showed enthusiastic appreciation as he picked up his rope and gave them a smile, but he hadn't done enough for the win. He was looking at third place, maybe fourth.

This was Paulo's night.

On the other hand, Rowan had smiled at him.

SHE FOUND HIM packing up his kit, getting ready to roll, and figured she had about five minutes before her father started wondering where she was. Five minutes in which to say hey, and shove a wad of money at him. Money he'd used to buy clothes she still hadn't worn.

The 'hey' part of the conversation went well enough, but the money part went wrong from the outset. She held out the roll of greenbacks and his eyes went flat and hard and he got that stubborn look about him. Same look he gave every bull he rode.

"No," he ground out. "You want to avoid me all weekend, that's your prerogative. I got the memo. But let the time before that stand. You don't owe me anything."

Which left her closing her fingers around the roll of cash and shoving her hands in her jeans pockets for good measure. "You rode well," she said. "Best you could do on that bull."

"Maybe I'll draw a Harper bull next time. I still have a score to settle with *Over Easy*."

She nodded. *Eggs* had made short work of the cowboy on his back this weekend, drawing plenty of attention from both cowboys and tour officials. It was too early to say, except that her father was already saying it. They had a new, young, unridden champion bull on their hands, and that was a very good outcome for any stock contractor.

"I have to go," she said, glancing back toward the Harper truck currently taking up space in the loading bay. "But when you do ride that bull, don't forget to collect on that bet."

"Rowan—"

She turned.

"You trucking that bull to Charlotte next weekend?"

She nodded. "Yes."

"Good," he said. "Bring the dress."

CHARLOTTE CAME AND went without a win and without him riding the Harper bull he'd staked their date on. It got around, no fault of his, that he and Rowan had bet a date on him riding the bull and he wore the teasing of the other cowboys with equanimity. Growing up with four brothers had been good for something after all.

Rowan, who'd grown up with no siblings at all but who'd been traveling the circuit since she was small, paid no mind to the teasing either. These days if she saw Casey around she'd make an effort to talk to him. They got into a habit of sitting a rail together, way back behind the crowd at the chutes, and discussing the pros and cons of the bulls he'd drawn. She predicted the shape of the ride more often than not, and damned if Paulo and Huck didn't want in on those conversations too, and then it was all four of them sitting back and talking beforehand or afterward and benefitting big-time from the information exchange.

Rowan was flank man, or woman, more often these days, although her father was never far away when that happened and neither was Jock Morgan's son, Mab. Casey had no idea what the deal was between the two rival stock contractors other than Joe Harper had taken the boy under his wing and was teaching him the ropes and that Jock seemed to be around less and less. Rowan too was picking up some of Jock Morgan's slack but her lips went tight and she shook her head when he quizzed her on it.

"My father owes him one," was all she'd say. "It'll sort itself out."

"Not before you run yourself ragged."

"What's a few more bulls to put in the chute? Anyway, Mab's coming on. Pulls more than his weight now."

And that much was true.

Casey went home in the long break between Charlotte and St. Louis and became Tomas again, fourth of five sons, but it wasn't the same without his father there to settle differences and scores. His two oldest brothers were feuding over the way things should be run, Jett was competing in ski races in Europe, and Seth had half a dozen building projects in full swing.

It had taken Casey all of five minutes to figure out that his mother was barely holding it together, and that her distress resulted largely from the ongoing argumentative wankery between Mason and Cal—both of whom believed in their God-given right to step into shoes neither of them could ever fill.

He brought it up with them out in the barn, far away from their mother's watchful eye, and squared his shoulders when two sets of hostile eyes swung his way.

"Oh, and I suppose you can run this place better than either of us, college boy?" This from Mason, his oldest brother.

"Maybe I could, but that's not the point. I've always known this place wouldn't support us all so I've made plans elsewhere, and, yeah, it involves more study. So what? Not as if I've ever asked *anyone* here to pay for it. I make my own way. All I'm asking is that you respect our mother enough not to start a turf war. Can you do that? Or do I have to take you both on?"

"Testy," said Cal. "Probably not getting laid enough."

"He didn't win last weekend either," said Mason. "Vicious cycle."

Testosterone had to go somewhere.

He got in the first punch. And maybe his brothers weren't trying all that hard to put him down or maybe all the prep he'd put into getting fit to ride this season and all his workouts in gyms and boxing rings along the way had made a difference, but he also got in the last punch several grueling minutes later.

He'd pulled his punches, more or less. They all had.

More or less.

"I covered every bull I rode last weekend," he ground out between gasps, and, okay, maybe he was groaning on the inside and only just standing up but they were listening to him now instead of mouthing off. "I brought home seven thousand dollars and change in prize money, and now I get to listen to you two mock me for it while I put my head down and do whatever shit job you want me to do for the next two weeks of my break."

He caught Mason's gaze and kept right on glaring. Screw them both; he deserved to be heard. "What gives either of you the right to act as if you own the place when you don't? What gives you the right to give me grief, and Jett grief, for making our own way? I'd like to see you win Olympic gold or handle all the press interviews and charity appearances the way Jett does. I'd like to see you work all year toward earning a place at the pro bull-riding championships in Vegas and then turn your back on it because your family decided they couldn't, or *wouldn't*, change funeral plans to suit you."

Could be he had some latent anger about that that he needed to get a handle on. "Instead you sit here in paradise arguing over who's gonna run this place while the woman who raised you sits in the kitchen worrying herself to tears because you're not getting on. I'm fucking ashamed of you both!"

And now *he* sounded like their authoritarian father. Dear God, the madness was catching.

"Figure your shit out," he grated and headed back toward the house, but not before stopping to turn on a faucet and run his hands beneath cold water for a while. Keep the swelling down, get the blood off his knuckles. He needed his hands in order to ride and he needed to ride in order to get out of here. He loved this valley and everyone in it, but some days it strangled him. The expectations here that were set in stone. The roles each of them were destined to play.

The way so many people relied on him to keep the peace, *create* the peace, damn well *enforce* the peace when he had to—only somehow, in some twisted way, that peacekeeper role came at the expense of people thinking him the weak one. The one who could be pulled this way and that; the one who'd listen when others had had enough. The one who'd bend and never break.

He wasn't weak. He never had been.

But every man had a breaking point.

His mother was at the wood-fired stove when he came in, pouring coffee into a blue mug with a chipped handle. Her hair was steely gray and she'd lost weight since he'd last been home. She was still adjusting to life as a widow, still adjusting to being the head of a corporation that had a seven-figure turnover. She'd been a Southern belle once, before James Casey had swept her off her feet and brought her with him to this valley. She'd borne five sons and put down roots and made this place her home, but sometimes of late he wondered how long she'd stay now that she was alone. She had sisters down South. Her mother was still alive.

"The tour heads south after the Easter break," he began, and doggedly began to set out a different way forward to the road she'd been traveling. "I was thinking we might travel together and I could drop you off in Louisiana and you could go visiting. Pick you up again on the way back. Get a place down there, even, for a month or two. Use it as a base." It wouldn't be much but he'd make sure it wasn't a hovel either. "Just a thought."

"Want one?" she said, gesturing to the coffee, and her soft Southern twang, even after all her years living in Montana, still soothed his soul.

"Please." Guess that was a no on her heading south for the season.

"How'd it go last weekend?" she asked. "I couldn't watch. I just couldn't. That sport …"

She hated it. She'd always hated it, even more than she hated Jett's speed-demon ski racing and the extreme heli-ski tours Jett took tourists on. They were similar types, her two youngest boys. He and Jett had always enjoyed pitting themselves against something bigger and stronger, be it beasts, the elements or older brothers. "I came fourth. Didn't get hurt. It's early days and I'm not pushing too hard. Just looking to get from one event to the next with enough points in my pocket and no damage done." It was a long game, bull riding. To get to the end of the tour and still be in top physical and mental condition required more try, luck and dogged determination than a lot of cowboys had.

"That's good." She took a sip of her coffee, but maybe it was too hot because she turned and added some water from the faucet to it. "Did you talk to your brothers about getting on with each other?"

"Yeah, Mama." His moment of receiving maternal attention was over. "I did it just then."

"How'd it go?"

"Real good." They were probably together somewhere, over beer, dreaming up ways to try and destroy him. "I left them with a common cause."

Best not to dwell on his most recent methods for peace creation.

Overall.

ROWAN HARPER HAD it all. Enough prime Wyoming grazing land to expand the business twice over. Thirty years' worth of superior bucking bull genetics in the bulls on the ground and all the cowboys required to run the place. She didn't need to be out there with them working every day. Her father had never asked that of her, she'd simply tagged along as a kid, determined to make herself useful. He'd taught her as he went, almost as an afterthought.

And now she was all grown up, full of knowledge and opinions about bull breeding that occasionally got heard, and not another woman in sight to teach her the other things—like how to put on makeup or flirt with dark-haired bull riders with green eyes and wicked smiles that promised good times and more good times.

It was nine thirty in the evening and her father was asleep and Rowan was in her room, with her dress on and her boots on and nowhere to go, and a tube of mascara in her hand. One eye looked good and the other eye looked like she'd been in a fight and who was she kidding? She needed makeup lessons from girl-friends she didn't have—the Internet directions simply weren't cutting it.

She had an ache in her heart and an ache in her loins and the temptation to do something about it was strong. She'd had Casey's number since he'd taken off last year, and how she'd come across that had less to do with asking and more to do with outright theft of tour information, but the phone was in her hand and she dialed the number before she could change her mind.

He answered on the third ring and she should have hung up. Instead she said hello and gave him her name and the silence after that was deafening.

She was phoning for no reason. Didn't have a thought in her head, and who could make conversation out of that? "What are you doing?" she asked instead.

"Looking at my hands," he answered.

"I've done that. Although possibly not for the same reason."

"They're all busted up."

"Oh. Same reason, then," she said, and relaxed a fraction when he chuffed a quick laugh. "I'm wearing my dress," she said next. "And my boots. I figured you should know."

"Where are you?"

"In my room. It's a practice run."

Silence again, then: "So how's it going?"

"The mascara needs work. I haven't tried the lipstick yet. I'm not sure red's my color. Not without practice, at any rate."

"I hope you're not expecting my help there."

"No, but I'd like praise for trying. Can you do that?"

"Always." He sounded so warm and sure and she settled back against the pillows on her bed, boots and all, and crossed one knee over the other the better to observe them. It wasn't as if they were dirty. They were straight out of the box.

"Which boots?" he asked.

"The red ones. The brown ones make me taller and I love the round toe but the red ones are bold and make me feel reckless."

"And how does the dress make you feel?"

"Lost," she confessed. "I love it, don't get me wrong. I want to wear it out. But there's a confidence issue."

"What if you were somewhere no one knew you? Would that make it easier?"

She thought about it. "Would I be alone?"

"Probably not for long," he said dryly. "But for the sake of fantasy, pretend that someone you know is with you. Someone you like and are comfortable with. A friend."

She didn't have any of those.

"What about Gisele? The ones with identities of their own who bring something other than admiration for bull riders to the mix."

"Okay, I'm making up an imaginary friend," she said. "She comes from Brazil, her family grows oranges and she's a well-known portrait painter. She talks to me about artwork I've only seen in books but I like her anyway because she never makes me feel stupid. I wish she existed."

"So you're at a gallery opening of a friend of hers, in Brazil," he said. "And you're wearing your dress and those red boots and everyone there wants to know who you are because you're unique and they've never seen the like and they're interested. When you say you raise bucking bulls for a living and take photos on the side they're doubly interested. You could have any one of a dozen men. What do you do?"

"I look for you." The words were on the tip of her tongue, and she let them fall.

Silence. "I'm not there," he said at last, and it seemed as if the words were reluctantly said. "What do you do?"

"You bought the dress. Why aren't you there?"

"I gave you the tools. You did the rest. Figured out what you wanted and how to make room for it in your life and went for it."

She was still looking for him. "Oh," she said. "How did you bust your hands?"

"I don't want to talk about it," he offered gruffly. "Nothing to be proud of, though."

"Tell me about college," she said next. "How was it?"

"Easy in some ways, hard in others. I was used to sharing space but I didn't fit. I was more used to doing, rather than thinking. Climbed the walls on occasion. Got into bull riding when I blew off an assignment to go to a rodeo. A guy I'd gone to school with was there. He loaned me his gear and I signed up to ride. I went back to college more relaxed than I'd ever felt, and with enough cash to see me through for a month. I wasn't born to it, I wasn't bred to it, but hell I needed it. And it wasn't just for the money."

"It's the challenge. There's nothing like it. The focus. The danger. The adrenaline dump running through you at the end."

"How long since you last rode?" he asked, and now it was her time to be quiet.

"I—a while. I got hung up here at home a year or so back. Cracked ribs, a punctured lung, ruptured my spleen and ended up in hospital awhile. My father fired three men over it, including our foreman who'd been with us for fifteen years. I haven't ridden since."

The boots suddenly looked garish and she uncrossed her knees and drew her legs down the better not to see them. Confidences like that should never be spoken, and if they were they should be glossed over as soon as possible.

"Which bull was it?"

"One of our younger ones. I thought he was going to be

good, you know? He could buck, and he was one of mine, the bloodlines I've been using, but he never made it on tour. He was a little too interested in killing people. My father had always thought so, but I couldn't see it. Didn't want to see it. Turns out my father was right all along. Lesson learned."

"And you were the wreck. It turns my stomach."

"Because I'm a woman?"

"Because bull riding's a coliseum sport. Death is always in the wind. Doesn't matter who goes down, my stomach churns until they get back up."

Hers too. "Anyway, I don't ride anymore and on the whole I don't miss it."

"Here's a question. Would you let your daughters ride?"

"Yes," she said and closed her eyes. "Sheep first, then steers. I'd start them young. Train them right. Same way I was trained."

"I don't know if I could let them," he said.

"That's the thing about children—sooner or later they'll find a way to do what they want. Letting them has nothing to do with it."

Silence again.

"I'm a full partner here in the business," she said. "Half of everything is mine, and it's a lot, and I'd appreciate if you kept that to yourself. I don't even know why I'm telling you except that I need you to know. I also need you to know that I'll never cash out." She couldn't see her way clear of this life. Her family unit was too small. Unlike Casey's family situation, there was no one else to inherit, no one to pick up the slack.

"I won't mention it," he said gruffly, after a long pause. "But for what it's worth, people have already figured where you stand and what you're worth. I know well and good that I'm never going to match you for money or possessions. Maybe you think less of me because of it."

"I don't. Maybe you think less of *me* because I don't have much of an education."

"Education's about information. You probably know more about genetics, animal breeding and bull riding than I do. And photography." She could hear the smile in his voice. "Want me to tell you what I own?"

"Yes," she murmured, and picked up the other lipstick she'd bought last time she'd been in town. This one was a soft beige-pink. She'd liked it in the shop when she'd drawn a line of it on her inner wrist like the Internet tutorials had told her to. Now not so much. "I want to know more."

"I have a log cabin in the mountains that I rent to hikers over summer and skiers during winter. It comes with not enough land to run a horse but it's mine free and clear, and maybe one day I'll sell it or maybe I won't. And while I'm motivated to make the money I need to get the education I want, I'm not motivated to make money just so I can buy stuff. I don't want the big spread. I don't want to be tied down. I want to see more of the world and everything in it, not less."

"Bull riding's good for that. You could go to Australia and Brazil." He fascinated her, this man.

"I've already been to both."

Oh.

The wanderlust was strong in this one. He was telling her that up front.

"If I went out with you to dinner, where would it lead?" It was a question she'd been tossing around ever since he'd kissed her.

"Judging from the kiss we shared it'd probably lead straight to the nearest bed."

"And after that?" She wasn't saying no. She hoped he realized that. "What happens at the end of the tour? When you leave?"

"I ask you if you want to come with me, you say no, and we walk away with battered hearts and a pocketful of fine memories. That's how I see this going, Rowan. No lie."

"So why would you still want to do it?"

"Did I mention the memories?"

"Yes."

"And the personal growth and exploration?"

He hadn't mentioned that. "Sounds painfully won."

"The fun," he said next.

"You're not exactly one of the fun-loving cowboys on the tour," she reminded him. By and large he kept his alcohol consumption low and he didn't screw around. Not that she knew of, and she *would* know.

"I do like to keep my fun times private," he said. "Nothing wrong with that."

"Do you think we could keep others from finding out about any fun times we might have?" she asked, and he was silent for a long time.

"You mean your father," he said at last.

"I mean everyone."

"You want to keep me a dirty little secret?" His words came a lot faster this time.

"I don't want people to pity me once you're gone," she corrected.

"Why would they? Most everyone I know would be calling me the fool, not you. And they'll be taking their cue from you. It *is* possible to take up with someone and let go later and still be friends."

"You read that somewhere, did you?" She recapped the pinky-beige lipstick and tossed it in the wastepaper basket. Score. "Have you ever done it?"

"No."

She smiled wryly. "So we've established that you're not a love 'em and leave 'em fun times individual and neither am I. Beyond that, I have family expectations to consider, ones that don't dovetail with the kind of future you want to pursue. Beyond *that*, I don't want to get a reputation for screwing pretty cowboys, because that's not going to go down well with management and they barely tolerate me as it is. You might also want to consider that if you don't treat me right my father will skewer you, or at the very least make your life miserable. We're doomed."

"But the kissing was good."

"You were high as a kite at the time."

"The kissing was exceptional. We should do it again. Not to mention you're phoning me out of the blue and I don't recall giving you my number."

"Yeah, well. The kissing was good."

Chapter Five

Phoenix, Clovis, Reno, Salt Lake City. Runner-up here, third place there, always in the top four or five and it wouldn't be long before a buckle went his way, Casey could feel it. Sometimes Ro was there with Harper bulls and sometimes not. He wanted to ride *Over Easy* for the full eight seconds and collect on that bet that sat there between them, but he hadn't had that chance yet. All he could do was rack up points and collect his money and keep going. He hadn't been home in over a month—no point when he was so far away.

Arizona, Nevada, Utah, and the air tasted different here. Dustier, hungrier, and so was he. Less forgiving when the rookie who'd replaced Troy—an Australian rider—went and got hung up. Vicious in his appraisal of what had gone wrong and what could go still wrong if the rookie didn't work on getting bad riding habits gone.

He rang his mother every Monday. Called his older brothers as little as possible. Jett had won again in Switzerland and was well on his way to winning another world championship. He called Jett on a far more regular basis, and some of it was pride in his brother's accomplishments and some of it was reciprocal support for how Jett had stood up for him and argued hard and loud for Casey to ride last year in Vegas and for their father's funeral to be postponed for a week.

Jett had damn near come to blows with Mason over it, before finally backing down. *Only* backing down when Tomas had caught him by the arm and shouldered him backwards. There was no point arguing. It was three against two.

Their mother had been crying.

This being Casey's last tour, he took extra pleasure in the little things. The cheap motels and the fancy ones, the breakfast diner with the best sausages and eggs he'd ever tasted. He savored them because he didn't know if he'd ever travel this way again, and it was bittersweet, because a part of him loved this carney lifestyle. The people he caught up with every weekend or every other weekend were family, of sorts, and he'd miss them.

And there was Rowan, when he got to Cheyenne, and she was wearing the red boots and that sweet little pale gold top with her jeans, and she was drawing looks from all around because it wasn't her usual attire but it suited her and she was confident about it, and she was so, so beautiful.

She had no idea.

He rode like the devil that weekend, and when the preliminary scores were in he was first in line to pick a bull for the short go and *Over Easy* was it for him. He had a score to settle and a bet to win.

"I need your advice," he said when she came up to him in the hours before he rode again. "Tell me how to ride that bull of yours again."

"Ride left handed. You're the only one who's ever come close to riding him. The average time for a cowboy on his back is two point six seconds, that's if you don't include your ride. He's not interested in you once you're on the ground—I promise you that. He'll change direction on you, he did it last time at the six second mark and that's when he threw you. You were too far back in the pocket. Stay forward, stay tight. Forget the showy moves. Ride him for the duration and you'll get your points regardless. That's my advice."

"And dinner afterwards?" Casey said, within full hearing of half a dozen riders.

"You pick the place I'll pick the wine."

And if that wasn't incentive he didn't know what was.

Both Paulo and Huck were there to help him get set. Paulo had missed the final round. Huck was riding in it but was at the bottom of the pack rather than the top of it.

"This one's yours," Paulo said as Casey got set.

"That so?"

"I'm praying for you, my friend," Paulo said next. "I want to say I was here when you rode this malparido."

They got him set and *Over Easy* stood there like a lamb throughout. Paulo took his hand from Casey's vest to indicate that Rowan had tied the flank strap but Casey could already feel it in the movement of the bull beneath him. Casey gave the nod.

And *Over Easy* exploded out of the gate.

Time slowed between one second and the next. It felt like forever and he barely drew breath but his center line never failed no matter what that son of the devil threw at him. He kept in tight, just behind the bull's shoulders, raked when he needed to, and when that bull changed direction he was ready for it.

When the horn sounded he was ready for that too. Loosening his rope and looking for the easy exit, and *Over Easy* gave him one. Plenty of air on this dismount too, but he landed on his feet. This round was his.

He swaggered from the arena—there was no other word for it—up to an empty chute and over it, last ride of the night and the best, and Rowan was there, sitting a rail, witness to it all, and he smiled slow and sure. She shook her head and smiled right back, and then Paulo was thumping him on the back and near breaking a rib. Several other cowboys were congratulating him, and he thanked them, but his attention barely wavered. Cheyenne was his. The buckle was his.

And Rowan ... well. He was at her service.

"Please tell me you booked a room at the hotel," he said, once the presentation was over and the press had been and gone.

"Room 1101," she said. "I've no idea where we're going but I'll be ready an hour from now."

Rowan's father waylaid him on the way out of the arena. Casey expected no less, but he wasn't in the best frame of mind to address the other man. Too much adrenaline from the ride still in his system. Too much want and not enough patience.

"You hurt her, I'll hurt you," the older man said, and meant every word of it.

"I understand." And then he'd stepped up close and let his own thoughts be known. "You give her no choice. This life is all she knows. Me or someone else, it's going to be a bull rider who claims her because you don't let her know any other life. That's on you, not me."

Old man Harper let him go without another word. But Casey felt the hate between his shoulder blades, all the way to his truck, and it gave him pause.

He could pull back on her now, minimize the damage done, see her to the door of her room at the end of the night and make her father and all who protected her happy.

And then he thought of Rowan at breakfast, bolting her food before belatedly realizing her manners and flushing. Rowan wearing gloves now when she worked. Rowan in her room, trying on the boots and the dress she'd bought, and the courage it had taken take to go against all she'd ever known and explore that side of herself. To admit that she was struggling.

Growing pains, of a sort.

He had no idea what she wanted the end result to be but damn he wanted to help ease her way, and if that meant putting up with her father's glares and tour management disapproval so be it.

Dinner it was and more if she wanted it.

Nothing he couldn't handle.

He told himself that all through his shower and afterward, when he swapped his jeans for fine dress trousers and a soft cotton dinner shirt that was white with a gray stripe. The buckle he'd just won stayed on the hotel bench and he opted instead for a black belt and plain silver dress buckle. This wasn't about winning the event and claiming the girl. It wasn't about the bet or finally riding Harper's rank bull. It was about *Rowan* and that intangible something that drew him ever closer.

He felt unaccountably nervous as he knocked on the door to her hotel room. As the door opened every thought in his head fled.

She'd worn the dress and the brown boots and her hair fell in soft waves to frame her face and rest lightly on her shoulders. She wore makeup too, first he'd ever seen on her and it was light and barely there as far as he could tell, but the things it did to her eyes and lips almost felled him. Eyes big and brown, lips pink and moist, and he had no idea how he was going to get her out through the hotel foyer without stopping the rodeo world dead.

"I made reservations for a steakhouse not too far from here." Heaven help him he was practically stuttering. "They say it's a good one."

"Sure. Let me get my purse."

She wouldn't need it. Way his luck had run this weekend and what with a thirty thousand dollar check in his pocket, he was buying and wouldn't hear otherwise. But it wasn't wise to go out without a wallet, or a purse—a way to get home or get help if something turned sour. Independence was important and he'd never deny Rowan hers.

"Do you have a coat?" he asked, and watched her eyes cloud over with dismay. Maybe she didn't have a coat to match the dress. Maybe that was a different shopping trip and one she hadn't conquered yet. "Not that you'll need a coat. It's a warm night and you're welcome to borrow my jacket if it turns cold later." Coat or no coat, she was going to turn heads. "You're beautiful."

"Not too much?"

"No. 'S perfect. All of it." Her. "You ready?"

Before she changed her mind and decided he wasn't nearly perfect enough.

The hotel foyer experience was fully as bad as he expected it to be. Cowboys Rowan had known for years stopped in their tracks to stare. From the minute the elevator doors opened, all the way past the open bar area, Casey made sure his eyes telegraphed a silent message. Make Rowan feel uncomfortable in her pretty, floaty dress that suited her to perfection and he'd make sure that discomfort was widely felt. Catcall, whoop or make a fuss and he'd eviscerate them.

"I, ah, should probably say something to my father," she muttered. "We won today too, and I haven't congratulated him yet."

Of course her father was sitting at the bar along with several others—every last one of them tour officials. Bull fighters Frank and Ben—Casey had the utmost respect for them. Jesse Keener, one of the announcers. Jesse who generally followed the show script to perfection, but when he strayed he did it in service to being wickedly funny. Alicia Flores, who headed up PR for the tour. Alicia's eyes widened and her gaze swept from Rowan to him and he thought he saw her shake her head in warning. No, keep going.

And then Alicia pinned on a welcoming smile as she got to her feet and took both of Rowan's hands in hers. Then came the scrape of chairs as everyone in the party stood and shuffled and gave greeting. Casey's handshake with Joe Harper was brief.

"It was a good ride," Joe said, and then turned his attention on his daughter.

"Oh, but let me look at you." Alicia wasn't letting go of her claim on Rowan anytime soon, and maybe that was a good thing. "I do believe every cowboy here is in shock at the sight of you in a dress. Shows what they know. You're absolutely exquisite. And your skin... I understand now why you cover up when you work." The older woman's gaze slid toward him. "You're looking very fine too, Casey. Winning looks good on you."

"Yes, ma'am."

"Where are you off to?" Alicia kept the conversation easy as others looked on.

"Steakhouse," he said.

"Casey and I had a bet from the beginning of the season," said Rowan, with a quick glance in her father's direction. "Dinner if he rode *Over Easy*. He's collecting."

"That so?" Rowan's father didn't sound impressed. "Who's paying?"

"I am. Sir." The *Sir* being just the right side of insolent. Or maybe not, if Frank's gleeful grin was any indication.

"Not that it matters," Alicia said smoothly. "I'm sure either one of you will be able to cover expenses, what with this weekend's good fortune. Casey, did you know Harper Bucking Bulls won the bull team challenge this weekend?"

He knew. He'd picked up close to thirty thousand for his win this weekend. Harper Bucking Bulls had pocketed a hundred thousand dollar check. "Celebrations all around."

"Rowan, we need to get together soon," Alicia said. "I'm after some more promo photos and beyond that I have an idea I want to run past you. Will you be around tomorrow morning?"

Rowan nodded.

"Good. Let's say ten tomorrow morning. I need my beauty sleep."

"What steakhouse?" Joe asked and Rowan sent her father a warning glance.

"Dad, I love you, I do. But if you turn up to the steakhouse we're eating at, with a party in tow, and crash my date—" her father winced at the word "—you and I are both going to regret it."

"Rowan, you don't know what you're doing," her father said gruffly.

"With all due respect, Dad, yes, I do. I'm heading out to dinner with a man whose company I enjoy. I'm wearing a dress, because that's what I want to wear tonight. This doesn't have to be a big deal unless you make it one."

Harper gaze clashed with Harper gaze. Blue eyes stony and brown eyes imploring.

"Dad, I'm twenty-four now, almost twenty-five," Rowan pleaded quietly. "C'mon."

In the end it was Joe Harper who nodded, but not before sending a vicious silent warning Casey's way. Casey, in turn, let it roll straight over him. There was a lot going on here and not all of it was his fight. Rowan was asserting her right to conduct herself as she saw fit and if she had to go against her father's wishes in order to so, so be it.

Funny thing about independence—only the person seeking it could truly claim it for themselves.

"Go. Be young. Enjoy." Alicia broke the silence. "I suspect we're settling in here for the evening. You know you're always welcome to join us later, after your meal. Or not.

Perhaps you'll go dancing."

Information wrapped in smiles. Loose plans and a clear warning not to come this way again tonight if he wanted to keep Rowan to himself. He nodded. Waited to see if Rowan was done, and then she turned abruptly, head down as she was wont to do, and bumped straight into Casey's chest.

It was only right that he put his hand to her waist to steady her.

"Damn, shit, sorry. I got lipstick on your shirt," she said, from somewhere around his pecs and then her fingers came up and she started rubbing and Casey stifled a sigh because this? In front of her father?

Wasn't helping her cause.

"It's okay." He caught her hand, and she looked up at him with apology in her eyes and he was toast. "It's nothing." His gaze flickered to her lips.

"Did I mess it up?" she whispered. "The lipstick. Do I need a mirror?"

Her confidence was wafer-thin. "No. You're good."

She nodded and stepped away from his hand, sending one last glance at the lipstick swipe on his shirt before ducking her head and automatically moving to put her hands in her pockets only to realize she didn't have pockets. Instead, she clutched the straps on her shoulder purse as hot color stained her cheeks.

Rowan's unease. Her father's glowering disapproval. Hidden smirks and not so hidden ones.

He'd had difficult dates in his time but none so difficult as this. "Ready to go?"

"Yes. Beyond yes."

Good enough for him.

He kept his hands off her as they headed through the bar, the foyer and out the hotel entrance. The valet had brought his truck around. He'd had it washed and polished and it glowed cherry red. Not exactly inconspicuous. Another reason for her father to think him a fool for driving such a gas-guzzling old-timer, but he liked it. It had been a gift and every last one of his brothers had worked on it with him over the years.

Fight with them, humor them, call them on their inconsistencies. Love them, make mistakes, and love them again. That's what families did.

He helped Rowan into the cab and shut the door behind her. The valet flipped him the keys and he gave the man a fifty.

Rowan was silent as he turned the key and set the engine to rumbling. He pulled away smoothly, knowing full well eyes were still watching from inside the hotel.

"That went ... well," said Rowan after a good five minutes of silence, and Casey snorted.

"Well enough." No punches had been thrown.

"I didn't think me wearing a dress and going on a date was going to cause quite so much fuss."

"Didn't you?" Surely she'd had some idea of how such a

transformation would be received. He shot her a quick glance and fell into thrall all over again at her delicate silhouette backlit by neon city lights from the cityscape beyond.

"I thought he was getting used to it, seeing me talking to you and hanging around with Paulo and Huck. Working as flank man some of the time. Becoming more a part of the tour in my own right and less of a … shadow," she finished quietly. "Guess not."

"Give it time."

"Yeah." She put her hands in her lap and played with a pretty ring on her middle finger. The stones were bright and big and probably cost more than his truck. "Did you ever have to fight for your identity?"

"Maybe as a kid I did. I was one of five, one of Casey's boys, but that didn't last long. We're all different. I was doing my own thing and going my own way when I was really young. Never wanted to follow in anyone's footsteps. Never wanted to be like my father, or my brothers, or anyone, really. I don't know how else to explain it. My upbringing wasn't like yours. I was left to be independent. Encouraged to make my own way. It's always easier to go where you're led."

"Tell me about your family," she said.

"All of them?" They'd be there all night.

"Maybe not all of them. The youngest one: Jett. I looked him up, saw some of his promo shots. Thighs like tree trunks."

Casey grinned. "He keeps threatening to teach me everything he knows about sponsorship and self promotion, which, admittedly, he knows a lot. The difference being Jett *likes* the limelight."

"He's not as pretty as you, though."

"Pretty? Seriously? You don't want to use the word *handsome* instead?"

"For you? C'mon. You're as pretty as cowboys come."

"I'm ruggedly handsome."

She smiled, warm and wide, and took his breath away all over again. "You keep telling yourself that, buckle boy. Prettiest face I've ever seen."

"The mirror's right there. And if you look in it I can fix that notion for you straight away."

"Me? I'm not pretty."

"What are you then?" Identity began with analysis of form, surely.

"Boyish. Thin. Plain."

"Mirror," he countered. "You really need to look in it."

"Lacking in confidence," she continued.

"Your father's one of the best stock handlers I've ever seen," he told her. "There's not one man on the tour who doesn't respect him for it. You're just as good."

"Mab gets more praise in one weekend than I've ever received," she replied. "I'm a woman doing what's traditionally a man's job in a man's world and as long as I shut up about it and keep my head down and don't draw attention to myself they'll let me keep doing it. The only reason I get more play in the back pens and in the chutes this year is because Jock Morgan's got cancer and Mab's not experienced enough yet to take his place. I take care of our bulls and my father takes care of Morgan's stock under the guise of teaching Mab a thing or two. Mab barely even knows his father. Jock skipped out on his wife and son fifteen years ago. Met up with them last year again and came away with a son who thinks the sun shines out of his ass."

"Ro." Casey's voice came at her quietly and wrapped around her soft and warm. "Are you jealous of the ride Mab's getting?"

"No." The hell she wasn't. "A bit. I like Mab, don't get me wrong. He works hard and he wants to learn."

"But?"

"He's male. I'm not."

Mab was coming home with them in the break because her father had promised to put the kid on some practice bucking steers, and she wasn't about to stick around and watch while her hand itched for rope she could no longer grasp. Some date she was turning out to be. Rowan cursed her insecurities and vowed to bury them instead. "Sorry," she muttered. "Let's change the subject."

"Did I ever tell you about the time I went camping up in the mountains with a bunch of wildlife conservationist Aussies and they thought I was a bear?"

Rowan blinked, and then smiled. Tomas James Casey, changer of subjects. "No, you haven't. Spill."

"There we were, five of us, with the Aussies sleeping off their jet lag and me up early and putting breakfast together and one of them woke and decided I was a bear, prowling around the camp. They then proceeded to have a ten-minute conversation about which one of them was going to come out and piss on me because one of them had read somewhere that urinating around the tent would warn bears away."

"Not if the bear was *right there*. Plus, that's more of a myth than a certainty."

"Indeed."

"Did they have guns?"

"No guns."

"So what'd you do?"

"Me? I kept throwing sticks at their tent for the next ten minutes, and occasionally grunting." He smiled angelically. "Like a bear. And then the girl who was with them unzipped the tent flap, stuck her head out and said, 'Casey, you bloody bastard, if you don't have breakfast ready by the time I get up you'd better believe not one of you is going to be pissing straight for a week.'"

"I like where this story's going," she murmured.

"I fell madly in love with her of course, but at eighteen

she was too old and far too wise for me at my tender age of fourteen. To this day they call me Big Bear. It's a sign of affection for an Aussie to give you a nickname. Possibly. Troy says it is."

"Troy? You mean the Wonder From Down Under? Breaker of hearts, defiler of innocence? The one with the well-developed death wish?"

"That's the one."

"And you believed him?"

"Troy's all right."

"I know. It's just … not many other people know that."

"He keeps it well hidden." Casey had the most devious smile on the planet. "But he does illustrate my point."

"You have a point? Do you want me to call you Big Bear?"

"My point is: it doesn't *matter* what other people think you are. That's their problem. Don't let their expectations contain you. Be you. And if you're just figuring out who you want to be, and it seems to me you might be, well, don't forget to have fun doing it. Try things on for size. See if they fit."

"You mean try you on for size."

"That is definitely an option, yes. I'm pretty, you said so yourself. I'm also buying tonight, not that you care. I'm in a good mood because I finally nailed that ride and the reward is you in that dress and that pleases me."

She stared at him loftily. "I am no man's *reward*."

"See? That's your identity speaking."

"Casey, I swear, if you don't stop tutoring me I'm going to make that girl from the tent seem like sweetness and light. You're buying." She had no problem with him buying or driving, but heaven help him if he kept on trying to analyze her or help her realize her potential. "There's going to be champagne and you're going to drink it with me. There may well be dancing. I may even try on some seduction skills for size. Do you have a problem with that?"

"No, ma'am."

If lazy enthusiasm was a thing, it was there in his smile and the appreciation in his eyes. It was the same appreciation he had when they were sitting a rail together during an event, or when he was standing back, watching her do her job.

It wasn't dress dependent and that was good to know.

The steakhouse was an upmarket one with white linen napkins and candles on the tables. The service was good, the menu extensive, and Rowan laughed when he ordered almost exactly what he'd talked about when he'd been concussed all those months ago. She ordered the BBQ smoked ribs and an extra napkin for her dress and resigned herself to getting sticky. Ribs were her favorite, and the meal—the waiter had warned her—was huge. Casey would probably clear his plate before she did and that would be good.

She hadn't forgotten wolfing down her breakfast in his presence.

She was a work in progress, and Casey had a way of accepting that. It gave her room to simply *be*.

"I've been talking to Alicia about some old photos I took years ago when I was messing around with a new camera," she said as their drinks and nibbles were served. "They're bull-rider based—sometimes it's just the arena during setup or takedown. Some of the pictures are black and white but there's years of them. Occasionally Alicia asks to use some of them for AEBR posters and postcards and the like."

"Makes sense." Casey's eyes gleamed in the low light, intent on her, listening to her, and boy, that was a hit and a half for her confidence and her libido.

"Want to have a look?"

He did, so she pulled her phone from the silly little handbag she'd bought to go with the dress and found the folder with the pictures. "They're a little bit bittersweet, some of them, but I think that's why she likes them. Not the glitz and the glory but everything that's going on underneath." The sorrow and the pain, those were the subjects she'd sought out back then and still gravitated toward. "Maybe I should group them by season and place. Santa Fe to Salt Lake City and three between, that kind of arrangement, add a few location shots to the mix and present them to her as a Year in the Life. A seasonal thing with highs and lows and changing colors and backgrounds. I always take arena pics when we first arrive. Year after year, I have so many photographs."

She handed him the phone and he pushed through half a

dozen photographs, and maybe some of the faces belonged to people he knew but most didn't. She hadn't chosen action shots of bulls and riders. She'd chosen quieter moments altogether, for the most part. A cowboy trailing his rope behind him as he limped from the arena. A hand going into a banged-up glove not a foot away from where a penned bull stood waiting. A rookie with hope not yet beaten from his body. An old-timer carrying too many miles and a body bowed with injury.

Rowan sat in her chair and tried not to fidget as Casey scrolled through the photos she'd chosen so carefully. It wasn't just the lives of the cowboys she was putting on show, this was her life too, long years of it, and if the smiling moments were altogether rare, well, maybe that was a reflection of her own feelings on the matter. There was an element of weariness to these photos—tucked in there right beside the beauty.

She wanted him to like them.

"There's none of you," he said finally.

"I was the one taking the shots."

"I know that." He nodded along. "And you're there in every shot. It's your story."

"I don't want to be the story."

He looked some more, went back and forward between pictures. "If it were me I'd want all those shots, not as postcards but together in a book, arranged like you said. Places and seasons. Feelings. The rhythm of the years. And

I'd want your story there too. I'd want to know what you were doing there too."

"I'd rather keep me out of it." Surely he of all people would understand her need for privacy? "You chose not to expose your family to the AEBR PR machine when your father died. You protected them and it doesn't seem like you regret it."

"I regret it a bit. Not riding in Vegas last year—that's a cut that hasn't healed fast." He made a face, a grimace. "Just ask my brothers."

"I don't have a Vegas to reach for. I have …"

"An identity to protect?" he asked quietly.

"Yeah."

"Your call." He handed the phone back. "They're good. There's a story there, more than one. Don't sell them short. Any of them."

He changed the subject to the little black bull-riding statistic books after that, and gave her something else to talk about, even if he did tease her about being a closet mathematician. There was food and champagne and laughter and always lazy, lazy appreciation in his eyes when he looked at her.

He made her feel good about messy ribs and bull stats for dinner. The bloodlines she was chasing. The battle between size, strength and agility and that all-important quality that both bull and rider needed to succeed. The try in them.

After the meal there were suggestions that had to do with

dancing and more dessert but that wasn't quite what she wanted. Neither of them had suggested returning to the hotel at this stage. Casey was probably picturing her father waiting for them in the bar, because Lord knows she was.

And then they were spilling out into the parking lot and Casey was opening the passenger-side door of his cherry red ride and lifting her up into the seat and pulling her close rather than stepping away, close enough for her thighs to rest either side of his hips.

"Smooth," she whispered against his ear and he huffed a laugh and drew her closer.

"I try," he murmured, right before catching her lips with his. He started off tender and coaxing, plenty of room for push-back or pause.

Gentlemanlike, and all that.

She fisted her hand in his shirt and deepened the kiss. She knew what she wanted from him tonight and slow, careful courting in full view of the family circus wasn't it. She wanted the adrenaline junkie version instead, the one where they let go out here in the darkness or holed up in some anonymous hotel room and stripped each other naked the better to learn what they were like together.

Kisses sweet and sticky like molasses. Touches hard and hungry or slow and soft. Casey's hair beneath her fingers—and it really was as soft and unruly as it looked.

Moving right along to the good bits, which were his mouth at her neck and the hard curve of his erection nudging the place between her thighs, and damn but she loved dresses because dresses rode up and allowed access, and, oh.

There.

Right there.

The rasp of denim-covered hardness against her panties, and she would have as much of *that* as she could stand. And maybe a little more.

"We could go somewhere," she gasped. "Another hotel. A different one." Bypass all that was waiting for them back at the tour hotel and simply concentrate on one another.

Not the best suggestion she'd ever made. She could sense his objection in the sudden stiffness of his body and the way he rested his head against her shoulder, as if looking for a reason to deny her. Or maybe he already had one.

"It's not that I don't want to acknowledge you," she said. "It's just—it'll make it harder, before we even *know*."

"Tell me what you need," he rasped and won her all over again.

"You and me and somewhere else." It was a cry from the heart. "No circus, just us."

He shuddered hard, and maybe he felt it as a blow and maybe he didn't. He never did say. Just kissed her hard and fast and then drove to a hotel that had a concierge and a lot of stars and checked them in under his name, flashing a black card and a dimpled smile, and maybe he was trying to impress or maybe he was simply seeing to their needs.

Harper Bucking Bulls had pocketed a hundred thousand

dollars this weekend by winning the bull team challenge. Casey had pocketed near thirty thousand. She'd pay him back when she got the chance. Wasn't as if either of them couldn't afford the room.

They got to the room and he opened the door and ushered her through, ever the gentleman. He tossed his car keys, wallet and the room card on the bench. The hotel room was like thousands of others, beige and brown and trying hard to be inoffensive. He was the boldest thing in it. Glittering green eyes that tracked her every move and a cocky stance that screamed come and get it.

"This what you want?" Nothing but challenge in him.

"Yes." As she draped her shoulder bag over the back of a chair and turned to face him. Easiest answer she'd ever given. Every last bit of corded muscle, every roll of his hips and the heat of his mouth on her skin. She wanted it.

"*How* do you want it?" he asked next, and now there was a question that required consideration.

She walked back towards him and put her hand to his chest and then slowly snaked her hand up and around the back of his neck and drew him down for a kiss, stopping just short of taking it. "Hard and fast to start." No point disguising her need. She wasn't a virgin and her day job was altogether physical. She wanted to feel him. "And then all night long," she whispered against his lips.

His clothes came off, and there were bruises to work around on his body and gasps to be had as her dress came off and he captured one of her breasts in his mouth. He was good at this, his hands sure and knowing, and she didn't begrudge him any of his knowledge or how he'd obtained it.

He had her on her back on the bed in no time, lips and hands trailing a path down her body until he got to where he wanted to go, shoulders parting her thighs and calloused fingers tracing impossibly soft circles around her throbbing clitoris. He put his mouth to her next, a broad swipe of a lick, and paused when she shuddered hard. "Yeah?" he asked huskily, seeking her agreement for liberties already taken.

"Yeah." Hell yes and pretty please and more.

He couldn't stop.

Give him a present and he'd unwrap it and claim it as his, nothing surer. Treasure it protect it, love it for all he was worth, because someone had taken the time to give it in the first place.

He had skeletons in his closet, plenty of them, issues unsolved, and he had Rowan Harper in his arms, waiting to be loved, and he could do it. Learn what she liked; lose himself in the way she responded to this caress or the other. Make it good for her.

The way she arched into him when he dragged his lips along her ribs, one, two, three and then the next. She wasn't skinny, she was compact, fit in his hand and he knew what he was doing thanks to a wayward youth. Pebbled nipples and an arch to her spine that was gratifying, and her hands—quick and sure. Perhaps she'd had a wayward youth too. Her hand on him, milking him, coaxing him, and he wanted more, always more with this woman.

In, and in, and there were condoms but she said no to them and he didn't protest. Sorted, she said, and it was warm and so tight, and her mouth was on his and it was scrambling his brain. Rowan over him, under him, pinning her, sheathed in her, and it was all-encompassing and more than he'd ever expected. The heat and the slick, hot need and utter abandon. He wanted this.

Took it with a shudder and a groan.

They finished with her on top, bearing down and riding hard, and he appreciated the effort, fingers tangled in her hair and his lips never leaving hers, hips pistoning, over and over, pleasure building.

"Please," she whispered, and "please," again as he turned them and put his fingers to her center and never strayed from his course. She was part of him now and they would finish together. He would see to it, needed it, there was no other way for them, all gathered up and waiting.

He could get used to this.

She tightened and spilled over a moment before he did, one heartbeat, two, and then he was spilling into her, tense in his pleasure when hers was wordless rictus and release, a gasp and a sob and he didn't know whose. Maybe his. Maybe so. Maybe he never needed another challenge in his life if he could have this, day in, day out. Rowan, naked and sated, sweat-soaked and his.

So much for taking his time with this.

He was done, gone and hers, and he figured it for a revelation he might keep to himself. Not cheating, just self-preservation, because who in their right mind whispered words of love to a woman on their first time between the sheets? Didn't want to scare her off, no pressure, just this, and, "Oh," she said, when she'd caught her breath and he'd moved off her a ways but not enough to let her go. "Oh, boy."

"Not a boy, Ro."

"Oh, I *know*."

And if that was praise he'd take it.

So there was that, and there was the promise of sleep and Rowan wasn't pulling away. They could go get cleaned up and head back now to the other hotel, best bet. It wasn't yet midnight, but he wasn't inclined to move and she didn't seem to have any ambitions in that direction either. The room was paid for until morning.

"Was there a plan in place to go back to the other hotel?" he murmured, and then got waylaid by the promise of her collarbone and his lips and the soft sound she made when the two met.

"No plans," she said, and that was good enough for him.

And then she kissed him and there was no more thinking.

CASEY

THERE WAS A solution to a walk of shame, decided Rowan the following morning, and it involved ringing down to hotel reception to see what time the clothes boutiques on the ground floor of the hotel opened, only to discover that the hotel had a handy clothes purchase plan that involved giving them her dress size and clothing requirements in exchange for them sending up a selection of clothes that were likely to fit. It could arrive with room service breakfast and the day's special was eggs over easy, bacon, pancakes and coffee, and if that wasn't a sign to just do it, she didn't know what was.

Casey was still in the shower when she said yes to it all and swapped his credit card that had secured the room over to hers. He wasn't paying for this, not this time, and she'd never been more glad to have money at her fingertips, hard-earned and rarely spent.

Breakfast came, and the rack of clothes came, and they ate while Casey laughed at the clothes. Maybe anonymous morning-after hotel-clothes shopping should be her thing, because the jeans were good and the tops were sweet designer tees in either a plum color or silver. The plum one crossed over at the breast and she chose it first and slipped it on. Casey's eyes darkened to moss and that was that.

She took the tag off and left it on.

It wasn't that she wanted to keep their night a secret. She just didn't want the whispers that came with spending the night with the guy who'd won the buckle. That wasn't them. That wasn't what this was. She wanted to *protect* this.

He understood. He said he did, at any rate, but as he pulled up where she asked him to drop her off, well short of the tour hotel so she could walk in, as if she'd been out to grab coffee or breakfast, she wasn't sure if he did.

"I'm not ashamed of you," she said and he said nothing, but there were storm clouds behind his eyes and a tightness to his features that suggested none of this sat well with him.

"But you're ashamed of what we did."

"No," she said. "*No*. It's just …"

"You don't want to commit to a relationship."

"It's not that either. It's complicated. I don't want to put you in harm's way."

"Assume I can take care of myself."

"I don't want to put *me* in harm's way," she said next. "I don't *want* to go from being Harper's daughter to Casey's woman. I want people to know *me*."

Silence.

"So I'll see you in Pueblo?" she said hesitantly. "We'll catch up then?"

"Yeah," he said gruffly. "Okay, yeah. We'll do it your way."

Pueblo, Colorado. Next stop on the tour.

Chapter Six

PUEBLO CAME AND went. He'd ridden hard this weekend and had the bruises to show for it, but he wasn't in the money, and his frustration was riding high on several fronts. The mediocre riding. Tour management's greater than usual demands on his time for meet and greets and local interviews.

Rowan.

Rowan had been there both days and they'd talked as usual, and she'd sat with him and Paulo and Huck, as usual, and she drank with them in the hotel bar afterward—which wasn't that normal but he'd take it.

She was staying with the bulls on a ranch outside the city limits and there was no sneaking away from there, or so she said. No turning up there on his part either. Not if they wanted to keep their relationship under wraps.

Rowan's call and he'd abide by it, and by God he hated it.

All he wanted to do was roll her beneath him and drive himself home. Spend time with her alone. Watch her wake up beside him, her hair a silken cloud on the pillow and her shoulder tucked beneath his.

She'd kissed him once this weekend when no one had been looking and it almost undid him.

He was over thirty years old and he felt like he was fifteen again and sneaking around stealing kisses from the preacher's daughter. There were too many eyes on him. There was no damn *time* to do anything except be restless with wanting and to sneak glances when he thought no one was looking, except there were people looking and Rowan's father was only one of them.

Alicia the sharp-eyed and Gisele the softly knowing. Jock Morgan, Mab's father, had taken to watching. Plenty of the other riders had noticed Casey's agitation and a fair number had guessed the cause of it.

He took their ribbing in stride. Not as if he hadn't dished out his share of it.

No point protesting this was different.

Even if it was different.

He spent his nights alone and restless and his days second-guessing every move he made.

There was no point staying down south after Pueblo, what with a three-week break before the next leg of the tour. Omaha, Deadwood, Billings—those were some of the stops coming up and they were practically in his backyard, not that anyone else in his family thought so. He could count on one hand the number of times his family had come to see him ride.

Jett had dragged their father along to Billings once. His brother Seth had watched him ride in Deadwood. Seth had been down that way already, hunting feature wood for a client. Casey hadn't come anywhere near the money that time, sprained his wrist instead, but they'd ended up painting the town red regardless. Too many beers spread out amongst a small band of rodeo brothers and one real brother who'd taken the time to come and support him. It was why Casey never said no when Seth was a laborer short and needed a hand. It was why he defended Jett's right to come and go and train and *live* the way he wanted to.

The sting of two older brothers with tongues that cut a little too deep and a habit of mocking other people's success was why Casey only lasted two days back home this time before taking off for the cabin. He said it was because he needed to make sure it was in good repair before the first of the summer hikers came through. He wanted to check for leaks, tidy it up, see what the melt was doing.

He needed to keep moving. If he was moving he didn't have to think about where he was going with Rowan and what he was doing.

He spent the first day at the cabin getting snow off the roof. Day two he started shoveling it off the porch and away from the doors. He lit a fire and chased the damp away, drove into Marietta and came back with enough non-perishable food to restock the pantry and the freezer.

Come dusk he stood at the door and looked out over the

valley and tried to pretend he didn't love it as much as he did. Tried to figure how he might one day get back here and be his own man, local livestock vet, breeding specialist, wildlife ranger. Something.

He thought of Rowan and her big brown eyes and expressive face. Pleasure or insecurity—everything showed on it, no wonder she wore a cap so often and tugged the brim low. Hid her perfect body beneath baggy, unisex clothes, although she was doing a little less of that these days.

When she wasn't working the back pens at the show she might these days show up for socializing, often with Alicia Flores, sometimes with Kit's wife Gisele. Still wouldn't be seen leaving with him, for all that she'd talk to him in public, spend time with him, favor him.

And screw with him in secret until they were both a quivering mess.

She'd be going on a road trip during the break, she'd said. Hunting down the last of the signatures she needed before firming up pictures for a coffee table bull riders book she and Alicia were working on. The AEBR were sponsoring it and held part copyright of some of the pictures. A Colorado publisher was doing the rest.

There was no money in it, Rowan had told him with a hint of defiance. The advance would barely buy her a new outfit, not that she needed one, because she now had three dresses overall, she'd told him. She was tackling the project because she got to meet new people far removed from the sport of bull riding. She was spreading her wings. Trying on new identities for size and liking the fit.

He'd always encouraged it.

He wanted her to fly.

She was taking a week-long photography course with some famous photojournalist or other soon.

Professional development course, she'd said, and there'd been that smile he knew so well because he had one just like it. Defiance in the face of opposition. She wasn't even expecting him to understand the opportunity she'd been given or the considerable amount of hard work and talent it had taken to get there.

Not expecting anyone to look close enough.

She was in Seattle this week. He knew as much because he damn well *did* listen during the foreplay and afterplay of their clandestine relationship. He listened to every word she said, never mind if he could barely keep his lips and hands off her. He listened because they were words spoken just for him.

When his phone rang the next morning, he wasn't expecting it to be Rowan. If she phoned, she did it in the evening from the confines of her bedroom or a hotel room. Wasn't her anyway, it was his mother's voice he heard and he closed his eyes and rubbed at the frown lines between his eyes, because his mother had been uncharacteristically quiet around him lately, all worried eyes and furtive looks and he didn't know why. He was all right. Doing well, all things considered. The woman he couldn't stop thinking about was treating him like a dirty little secret and he didn't feel good about that but he hadn't said no to any of it. He was quite prepared to own his bad decisions outright.

"Mom. What can I do for you?"

"Just wondering whether you're coming back down the mountain anytime soon."

"Wasn't planning to until Friday. Still doing some tidy-up. Cold got to the hot water pipes again."

"Can you make it any earlier? You have a visitor and she's here in my kitchen, nervous as a half-wild kitten and not real sure of her welcome. It pains me to say that I don't know enough about your social life to know whether you want her here or not. Her name's Rowan Harper."

He stopped dead, leaking water pipes forgotten. "Rowan Harper is sitting in your kitchen?"

"That's what I said. Who is she?"

"She's, ah—"

His mother waited, but he didn't know what word to choose.

"—she can be there. I mean, I don't mind that she's in your kitchen. I'm a little surprised, but it's not a problem. For me. Is it a problem for you?"

"Very lucid of you, Tomas."

He was getting there.

"What exactly should I be doing with her?" his mother asked. "Should I put out the good tableware? Offer her a bed for the night? Screen her for potential daughter-in-law status?"

What the hell? "Just give her a drink and keep her there. I'm coming to get her. And don't let Cal or Mason hit on her or I swear to God I'll relieve them of their teeth."

"Ah," his mother said quietly, and he didn't even want to know what an *ah* like that meant. "Well, I *was* going to point her in your direction but I will confess to suddenly having a burning desire to see you in the same room together. See you soon, Tomas. I'll make cookies."

"No, Mom. Send her up. That'll work." Rowan was country born. She'd find her way. The road wasn't that slippery. "*Send her up!*"

But he was talking to a dial tone.

ROWAN LOOKED UP from the bone china teacup that was so thin and fine she could see the outline of her fingers through it. The cup was full of tea and liberally laced with sugar but she'd put it back down almost as soon as she picked it up. What if the handle broke or something sloshed? What if Casey's mother could see at a glance the callouses on Rowan's hands? Callouses that never seemed to go away no matter how many times she wore gloves when she worked.

The kitchen she was sitting in was a cheerful, sunshiny place to be. Clean but messy, mainly because Casey's mother had been putting groceries away when Rowan arrived. Mail on the counter, pen and paper next to it. A lived-in kitchen in a regular ranch house, nothing fussy.

And nothing whatsoever like her own sparse, barely functional cooking space back home.

Casey's mother had left the room to call Tomas down from some ridge or other, where he'd been working, and when the older woman had returned... that's when the good china had come out and the madness had started and *what had he said to his mother about her?*

The kitchen table in front of Rowan was loaded with cookies the size of her hand. They were piled high atop a fancy serving plate, the kind people put on a sideboard in a formal dining room, and the teapot had real tea in it and the pattern on the outside of the teapot matched the pattern on the cup and the pattern on the milk jug, and the sugar cubes had a set of tiny silver tongs to go with it, and more cookies were in the oven now and the smell was making her stomach rumble, and Casey's mother with the Southern accent was insisting Rowan call her Savannah and *what was happening?*

Rowan had already disclosed the fact that she traveled the AEBR circuit as a stock contractor, and from that point on the older woman had peppered Rowan with questions about bulls, about life on the road, about Casey's riding, and about sponsorship. Questions a mother should already know the answers to, what with a son who'd been on the pro bull-riding circuit for the best part of the last four years.

Rowan's knowledge of what mothers should know about their grown sons was sketchy at best, but surely they should know more than sweet jack all?

And then the back door opened and at first she thought it was Casey, only it wasn't. This guy was dark-haired and well built but his face wasn't nearly as arresting. The cocksure swagger Casey wore so well was missing. The guy blinked at the table groaning with food and fine china but recovered swiftly enough to send her a nod as he grabbed a cookie. "Ma'am. Mom."

"My eldest son, Mason," Casey's mother told her. "Mason, this is Tomas's friend Rowan. From the bull-riding tour."

Mason came forward. He had a nice smile and a firm hand and his gaze was curious but careful too. Careful not to check her out. Wary for reasons of his own.

"Rowan's been telling me how sponsorship works," Casey's mother said next. "She says Tomas's main sponsorship deal was worth around ninety thousand to him last year."

Rowan saw Casey's brother wince out of the corner of her eye, but then he turned and headed for the kitchen and grabbed a coffee mug from the drying rack. When she turned back to Casey's mother, the older woman was staring down at her hands, her shoulders a little more rounded than they had been before.

"He's doing well though, this year," Mason said gruffly, without turning around. "Real well."

"If you could just *talk* to him about taking the money—"

"Not now, Mom. I'll get to him later." Brother Mason's gaze swung back toward Rowan, coolly aloof. "We have a visitor now."

Families were fascinating to Rowan. This one more than most.

"Yes, he's riding well. Tomas." She said his name aloud because he was Tomas here, amongst so many other Caseys, and she needed to get used to that. "He's pulling in prize money, maybe even enough to cover the sponsorship loss, but it's not just about money, you know?" Or maybe they didn't know. "His reputation took a hit when he didn't show for last year's finals. Part-time cowboy, they call him now. Ungrateful for the chances he's been given. He disappointed a lot of fans and even though he's back and riding well, not all of them are interested in getting behind him again. They think he's inconsiderate."

She met big brother Mason's hard stare with utter calm. "And don't get me started on how much trouble he was in with the tour managers for not showing up, and not telling them why until later. To be fair, I daresay he knew what he was doing. The AEBR's promo machine would have milked his father's death for all it was worth, so at least he protected you from that circus. But don't believe for one minute that he's not wearing that decision this season. Doors that were once open to him are now closed."

"The timing of the funeral couldn't be changed," big

brother Mason grated.

"Yeah, I figured. I'm sure you tried," she said and watched as a dull red flush crept across brother Mason's face.

Oh.

Guess they hadn't tried.

"Rowan's been telling me about her photography project," Casey's mother cut in hurriedly, and as far as a change of topic was concerned it was a good one. Rowan had most of the photos in a folder on her phone and didn't mind at all if people looked through it.

Rowan had pictures of Casey too, taken in Cheyenne and Pueblo before and after he rode, so she found them on her phone and passed the phone to his mother. Casey had known she was taking them but he didn't yet know that she wanted one of them for the book. His mother spent a long time looking through them, asking about one aspect of bull riding and the next. The way the draw was set up, the order in which the riders rode. The injuries and what it took to stay at the top and ride every other week and rack up the points, injured or not.

"Casey—er, Tomas," she corrected at two sets of blank looks. "Tomas was injured early this season with concussion, but was cleared to ride by the next event. A few weeks after that he dislocated his shoulder, but that's an old injury, and one he'll likely have to get seen to eventually—especially if he wants to keep riding left-handed the way he sometimes does." At more blank looks she tried again. "He's one of only a handful of cowboys in the competition who can ride both left- and right-handed, depending on the bull he draws. It's his left shoulder he tore. Doesn't he tell you any of this?"

Silence.

Okay, then.

"I like this picture," Casey's mother said, into the silence. "When was this taken?"

It was one of Casey—Tomas—sitting in the dirt with his back against a wall as he trimmed his rope and tried to pretend that his side didn't hurt like hell and that the bruise on his cheek and the split on his lip didn't exist.

"That was after one of our bulls, *Hammerfall*, raked him along a rail. He rode once more that day, and stuck his ride, and then the doc hauled him in for a checkup. There's a sports medicine team that travels with us. They mostly stop the guys from doing anything too stupid."

Casey's mother looked close to crying.

"No one's looking to deliberately make injuries any worse," Rowan offered hurriedly. "It's just … sometimes the guys would rather ride than be sidelined. Sometimes they *need* to ride because they need the points or the money. The adrenaline helps—lets them ride through the pain and walk away afterward. A bull puts Casey on the ground, he's going to want to pick himself up and walk out of the arena without help. It's part of the show. It's a matter of pride."

"He always did have a lot of pride," his mother said faintly. "Even as a little one, he never asked for help when he fell down. He always got back up, dusted himself off and kept right on trying to keep up with his older brothers. I had five boys under seven—and every last one of them a handful. There wasn't a lot of time or attention to go around, and Tomas was so self-sufficient."

"He got seen to," Mason said curtly. "Tomas is fine, Mom. He could have told us what he was giving up by not riding at the end of last year. He chose not to."

It was official. Rowan didn't like this brother.

Mason stormed out as Casey—Tomas—came in.

"Whoa," said Casey, and looked first toward his brother's retreating form and then at the table filled with all the beautiful things and the mountain of food and then his gaze sought hers and there was a world of confused apology in it. "What'd I miss?"

"Tour talk."

"You should have called ahead. I'd have made sure I was here."

She knew that now. Hadn't before. Figured she'd learned far more about him and his family in the short time she'd been with them in his absence than he ever wanted anyone to know. "That's true, and I'm sorry for not thinking to. It wasn't very considerate of me. I have two more photos to select for the picture book project and I haven't been able to get the signatures I wanted, so I thought I might use photos of you instead. I've come to show you the shots and get your approval."

He hovered by the door, and there might even have been a bit of wistful glancing in the direction his brother had gone, namely back out the door. And then he squared his shoulders and crossed the room, his hand gently caressing her shoulder and his thumb brushing the back of her neck as he bent and placed a sweetly gentle kiss on her lips.

"You know you're welcome here anytime." His mother could hear him. Anyone could hear him.

Maybe that was the point.

"Your brother made sandwiches," his mother said.

"I've already eaten." But he took a cookie and settled into the chair beside Rowan, and looked at the pictures, and nodded absently as she told him how she'd tracked down this person or that, and somewhere amongst the conversation when he said, "Can you stay a night? I have a cabin up the mountain," it was the easiest thing in the world to say, "Yes."

His mother got up and filled a basket for them after that. Food from the fridge and wine from the cupboard, and cookies and berries, enough for ten people, and when Casey protested his mother said, "Shush. Let me do this."

So Rowan watched as Casey stood back awkwardly, hands in his pockets, while his mother fussed. Rowan knew nothing about what mothers did for their children but this seemed ballpark. Food was love. And Savannah Casey was packing a lot of food.

Ten minutes later Casey followed Rowan out the door with the food basket in his hand and walked with her toward her ride. There was another vehicle parked next to it that hadn't been there earlier—a single-cab truck with a flat top and winch on the back—and he tucked the basket into the top corner and strapped it in.

"Sorry about that," he muttered.

"Sorry about what?"

"Whatever that was back there. With my mother and all the fuss. She's usually a lot more chill."

"I should never have come without calling ahead. That might have helped."

"Yep. Would have. What are you doing here, Rowan? I was under the impression that all you wanted from me was a tumble every now and then, and absolute secrecy about it afterward."

"I—yeah." She nodded jerkily. "I did. I do. Most likely. Or maybe not. I *really* should have called ahead." Or driven home another way altogether and not called in on him at all. "I can go."

"Not what I said." He leaned back against the side of the truck and shoved his hands in his jeans. "You sought me out. Surely you knew that if you came here I'd claim a relationship with you. This is home turf for me. My rules now, not yours."

He stood there with the eyes he'd inherited from his mother and those long, long legs. He wasn't huge around his arms and chest but what was there was all sinewy muscle. Enough strength to stick to the back of a bull with brute force, courage and skill. And then there was his sheer unbreakable will. This man did not let go if he wanted something hard enough, be it eight seconds on a bull or an answer to his question.

"So I'm asking again," he said quietly. "Why are you here?"

"I missed you. That's why I'm here." Once she got started it was easy to continue. "I wanted to know more about you. That's another reason I'm here." There was more. "I wanted to tell you I'm not trucking bulls to Omaha next week, so wouldn't be catching up with you there. That was reason three. Reasons four through eight had something to do with your kisses. I've mentioned reason nine already, in that I really do want to use two pictures of you and need your consent. Reason ten is that I'm done trying to keep what I feel for you a secret, and I *really* should have called ahead to see if you were okay with that, this being your family home and—"

His kiss came hard and hungry, and his arms at her waist were tight bands that held her fast, and she hoped to hell that his mother wasn't looking out the window or his brother wasn't over at the barn door looking out.

And then his lips gentled and his thumb caressed the curve of a rib and she gave herself over to saying hello in the way she'd wanted to ever since he'd walked into his mother's kitchen and looked at her and smiled.

"Get in the truck." He was lifting her up to make it happen, even as he spoke, and she wrapped her hands around his upper arms and her legs around his waist, which helped them not at all. "Where's your overnight bag?"

"Over there." But he was here standing right between her legs, so hard and warm, and she didn't want to let him go. She drew him down for another kiss and then another, and then he pulled back with a groan and shut the door on her once she was all the way in. There was a thud and the slightest bounce of the cab and that was her carryall stowed in the back, and then he headed for the driver's side door.

He drove with the careless competence that came of being put behind the wheel young and knowing the road to the extent that he could probably drive it while blindfolded. Snow had left the valley but as they headed up they encountered more and now the all-terrain tires on his vehicle made a lot more sense.

He was rock hard beneath his jeans, legs spread wide, his jaw clenched and there was too much space between the seats otherwise she'd have been tempted to rest her hand on his thigh and let her fingers track the inner seam of his jeans.

"How much further?" she said when they rounded a bend, and drove past a clearing surrounded by trees and largely hidden from the valley below.

"Five more minutes. Ever been parking?"

"No, my father kept me on too tight a leash for that." Especially after … yeah, Casey probably didn't need to know about her teenage crushes and the lengths she'd had to go to in order to evade her father's watchful eye. Her secretiveness wasn't a new development.

"Want to park now?" he asked, with a glint in his eye that promised deliciousness if she did. Always willing to help her out with new experiences, this man. What a giver.

"Does this mean you're something of a parking expert?" she asked.

"Four brothers and not a lot of privacy. We made do. That spot back there was particularly popular. You had to book it in advance."

She blinked. He grinned.

"Nothing worse than headlights coming around the bend when you're in the middle of something," he said.

"And were you often in the middle of something?"

"Me? No. Them? Always."

She didn't believe him for a minute. Tomas James Casey had game. And he was enjoying teasing her far too much.

"Your mother and Mason didn't seem to know what you'd given up last year when you chose not to ride," she said by way of ensuring she lasted five more minutes on the road without putting her hands on him.

The effect of those words was instantaneous. He shot her a hard glance before returning his attention to the road.

"I got the impression it was a touchy subject hereabouts. I may not have improved things." She didn't want to make trouble for him. Mostly, she wanted to confess her sins so they could get on with the earth-shattering sex.

"What did you say to them?"

"That it damaged your reputation within the industry and that tour publicity would have made a meal out of your father's death had you said anything. I never told you how much I admire what you did do."

"What did I do?"

He still wouldn't look at her, and she wished she was wearing her cap so she could pull it down low over her face and observe him more covertly. "You put your family's needs before yours. That's …" Not what I'm used to, she wanted to say. "I think that's love," she said instead. "I think more of you because of it. Not less." Never less.

"Yeah, well." Casey—Tomas—took one hand from the steering wheel to rub the back of his neck. She wanted her hand there, didn't know if he would accept it. Maybe it would feel too much like comfort. "Mason was the one who found him, the one who had to deal with all the red tape and the funeral arrangements. He wasn't tracking too well afterward. No one was. Better all around to help clear the path and get on with burying the man."

"Did you have a good relationship with your father?"

"It wasn't bad." He didn't say any more for a while and she let the silence stand. "We didn't always hold the same views; he could never understand my wanderlust or my need to prove myself somewhere else that wasn't *here*, but he knew I loved him. There was nothing left unsaid between us. Nothing I'm brooding on."

"And your mother? How are you with her?"

"What is this? Twenty questions?"

"I know nothing of mothers," she admitted. But that encounter back there between Casey and his mother hadn't seemed picture-perfect to her. "She packed us a basket full of food. That was nice. Welcoming. But before that there were fancy teacups and cake plates and baking. I'm not exactly sure what that was about."

"Don't look to me for answers. I try to keep my social life out of my mother's kitchen."

There it was again, a not so silent rebuke for tracking him down.

"Jett doesn't," Casey continued. "He hooked up with Mardie, who already has a baby girl, and my mother dotes on them all. Pretty sure they don't get the good plates although I suspect they get more cookies."

"Did you say something to your mother to make her think I needed the good plates?"

"No."

"Because back home, we don't *have* good plates." Her father had never worried about those things and neither had she.

"You're still living in your family home?" he asked, and now there was a question with a lot behind it.

"Yes."

"Ever thought about moving out? Having your own space?"

"I'm barely there as it is. Why would I want more space to not live in?"

"I'm wondering if you're ever going to be free to bring someone like me home and not have to get your father's permission first."

"I don't need permission." Not that she'd ever brought anyone home. "My house isn't like the one we just came from. It's not family space that needs protecting."

The house she lived in was a sprawling two-story ranch with far more bedrooms than people. Rowan occupied the east wing and had her own entry, kitchen, bathroom, laundry and living spaces. "Where I live … there's one roof but I have my own separate entry and living areas. My father has his on the other side of the house. In between there's a whole lot of common living space that no one ever uses. It's been that way since I was ten. So while I can't say my father would be happy if I brought a man back to the ranch, it wouldn't be as if I was inviting someone into his living room."

Casey was looking at her weirdly.

"Okay, I'm pretty sure my father would *try* to intimidate whoever I brought home, so there is that to consider. You've met the man. I doubt this is news to you."

"Since you were ten," he echoed.

"Are we having the same conversation?"

"You've been living separately from your father *since you were ten?*"

"It's the same house." They were definitely not having the same conversation. "It wasn't as if he didn't keep an eye on me."

"How? How could he *possibly* keep an eye on you when he was half a mile away doing his own thing?"

"Binoculars," she said, deadpan, but he didn't smile. "So I didn't have a mother who baked me cookies. I still got fed. I had a roof over my head." No need to mention those early years when she'd known without words that sometimes her father had wanted to pack up and *go* and leave her behind. Her father had never left her, no matter what his eyes had said. He'd always taken her with him, and she'd always done her best to not make him regret it. "Wasn't easy for my father, carting me around all the time. He had work to do."

"You should probably stop talking now." Casey's voice came at her rough and low. A muscle throbbed in his jaw and he kept his eyes on the road. "Unless you want my loathing for your father to be absolute."

"My father does his best by me. I don't hold grudges."

Casey had that air of implacability about him that he sometimes got before an especially tough ride. "I do."

They rounded a curve and the cabin came into view, rough-hewn log and stone walls, long and low, carved into the landscape rather than soaring out of it. But there were a lot of glass windows on show, some of them running from floor to ceiling. Not a cookie-cutter building effort.

"It's lovely," she said and it was even better inside.

Handcrafted, from the cupboards in the kitchen to the round fireplace that dominated the living room, it was an earthy, masculine, open-plan space, dominated by blue and tan furnishings and dark, plush carpet that her feet sank into as she made her way to the window.

The house looked over a different valley to the one they'd come from. It was more of a mountain pass than prime grazing land, but the view was spectacular and the mountains soared in the distance.

She turned to find him watching her, his very fine rear propped against the corner of the sofa and his hands in his pockets again. His look was keen and assessing and his smile was crooked. "Remote enough for you?"

"I do like the lack of neighbors," she said. "I've never been ravished in front of the fire in anyone's high-country cabin before either. In case you were wondering."

"Do you like it?" he asked, as if her answer actually mattered to him.

"Yes." It didn't quite have the lived-in vibe of the main house in the valley below, but no expense had been spared when it came to comfort and the furnishings and the cabin itself fit the location perfectly. "No deer heads mounted on the walls," she said.

"I rent this place out for part of the year. Tourists don't quite know what to make of them. Some like them; some don't. Me, I'm not big on death for pleasure, although I like taxidermy. It's a conundrum."

"So many big words."

"I'll shoot to protect. I won't shoot for sport. And I know you understand the big words."

"You say you want to be a vet," she said, and he nodded. "Have you ever thought about being a traveling vet on the tour?"

He looked as if he hadn't thought of it at all.

"You know the bulls; you know what's expected of them. Contractors have their own vets and animal whisperers, sure, but they're not always around when they need to be, are they? Just a thought."

"My reputation's shot," he said, with a shake of his head. "Not going to happen."

"Your bull-riding reputation is shaky. Your reputation for compassion and making tough choices is sound."

"Who are you?" he muttered. "You're like a secret weapon that clears away all the bullshit in your path."

"I have shoveled a lot of bullshit in my time," she said with a smile, and it was as if the sun rose over the mountains when he smiled back at her with no artifice, no deliberation, no knowledge of how good he looked doing it. It was a smile, freely given and she would have more of them. "What I meant to say was that I like what you've done with the place."

"My brothers helped build it. I went online and bought furniture. My mother online shopped her way through the kitchen cupboards—no flower patterns allowed—and I think she enjoyed it. I even have candlesticks. Somewhere."

"How many houses are there on the property?" she asked.

"Five, including the bunkhouse. There's a second family house that came with neighboring land my father bought years ago. One of my other brothers—he's a builder—he lives in that one. There's another cabin we built for practice but it's higher up and hard to get to. Jett uses that one when he takes people heli-skiing. And then there's this one."

Not a family who were scratching for money, never mind that that he'd freely admitted that the family property wouldn't sustain five sons.

"You talk about your younger brother a lot."

"He's hard to miss. Show-off, Olympic gold medalist, world champ, good guy. They say I'm like him only not."

"How not?"

"I refuse to use the word prettier, even though I am."

She smirked and ventured closer. "It's a word we all use around you. Take your lumps."

"He has drive and a will to succeed like you wouldn't believe."

"And you don't? Could have fooled me." Closer still. She put a hand to his chest and her lips to his cheek and he drew a shaky breath, not nearly as composed as he seemed. "What else?"

"He has a family now and I've never seen him happier. That … surprised me."

"Mm hm." He was so hard beneath her hands. So responsive.

"There's a competition to see who can buy the most outrageous hair ribbon for his little girl. I'm winning."

"Of course you are." The leather of his belt was well-worn and butter-soft beneath her fingers. "We should eat *after* the sex."

"I'm willing."

He really was.

Chapter Seven

CASEY WATCHED AS Rowan familiarized herself with the contents of his kitchen. He didn't know what was in half of his cupboards but she didn't know what was in any of them. She looked and he thought she liked what she saw of his home and the mountains around it, and she fit into his world in a way that made sense to him. She was of the land and born to hard work. Neglected as a child, not that she'd ever admit it, and ever so slightly daunted yet fascinated by traditionally female domains. Furnishings, kitchenware. Mothers.

Heaven only knew what she'd said to his mother.

He wanted her here, and on one hand that was a surprise and on the other hand it was no surprise at all.

He'd been trying to downplay his feelings for her.

No more.

They raided the food basket as the sky darkened to azure, bringing it down with them to the nest they'd made in front of the fire. She'd put on the new dress she'd bought on her travels and laughed at the approving look he'd given her. She'd kept to the caramel bronze colors and soft fabrics, because why mess with a good thing? But this one had turquoise ribbon below the shirred bust line, and half a dozen similar ribbons that made up the shoulder straps. When she sat and moved and reached for things they sometimes fell from her shoulders, and maybe he was a sucker for ribbon but he couldn't stop touching her.

"Why aren't you coming to Omaha?" he asked.

"Because I'm going to Denver to talk about printing paper for the coffee table bull riders book."

"Do you know anything about printing paper?"

"I know there are about a thousand types to choose from. They want a foreword from me. A snapshot of my life on the tour."

Her tone told him she wasn't any more inclined toward the idea than when he'd mentioned them wanting more of her story. "Told you."

"I don't want to do it."

He took a breath and let it out and the arm she'd rested on his chest moved with him. She liked tucking into him after sex, boneless and pliable. She liked it when he put his arms around her and let his fingers trace lazy patterns on her back, even if he worried that his hands were too rough for the soft delicacy of her skin. For someone so skittish about being around him nine-tenths of the time, she denied him nothing once they were naked. Not her thoughts or her reactions, not her feelings.

"People hear how my mother died and how I was raised

on the road and that bulls and bull riding is all I know and they get that look about them," she murmured. "The one that says child services should have been called twenty years ago."

"Do *you* think child services should have been called?"

"No. But I don't want to go back to those days either. Not even in my head. My father worked hard. Traveled hard too. Drank some. Especially early on. He's better now. But I don't want people to get the wrong impression if I say something that calls my upbringing into question. Something I don't even realize is wrong."

"Get someone you trust to look at what you write before you send it in," he suggested. "Or focus on how unique your upbringing was." There was a haunting melancholy to some of her photos, a despairing air to some of her down-and-out cowboys. "Bull riding's a tough sport. People expect big highs and devastating lows. You're part of that. Give them that in the foreword without getting too personal. You *can* pick and choose what you want people to know. There's always stuff we'd rather other people not know."

She pulled up onto one elbow, the palm of her other hand still resting on his chest. "Tell me something other people don't know about you."

"Then it wouldn't be a secret."

"I bet you had an idyllic childhood, full of rainbows and cookies."

"There were cookies." There'd been dark times too,

when he'd grown tired of being overlooked and unheard. "I ran away when I was six and took Jett with me. We were going to Alaska to save the baby seals. There'd been pictures on the news and I couldn't believe people could let that happen, and my eyes had started to water and a couple of my older brothers were teasing me about being a crybaby. So I whomped on them and Jett joined in and then my father came in and sent me and Jett to our room before we even had a chance to speak, and the injustice of it burned all night and into the next morning." He smiled to take the sting out of his words. It was a memory, not even that powerful. Young boys trying their alpha on for size, taking sides, and realizing the world wasn't perfect.

Rowan was smiling down at him, her perfect lips curved. "What happened the next morning?"

"Jett and I stole all the school lunches Dad had made, grabbed our coats and headed for Alaska. We got ten miles up the highway before one of our neighbors drove past and offered to give us a lift in the right direction. But he was heading home first so we went with him. By the time my father turned up Jett was fast asleep on the lounge and rancher Hicks was telling me about endangered species and wildlife conservation and I'd fallen in love with Bengal tigers. I never got to Alaska, but I did spend a lot of my childhood collecting and rehabilitating injured animals. Drove my local vet mad. I was there so often he ended up taking me on as a volunteer. Raptors were his specialty and he showed me a thing or two. You want to reset a broken bird wing, I'm your man."

"Huh," she said. "A runaway vigilante."

He smiled smugly. "If only my parents had glossed over that whole leading your brother astray and putting yourselves in grave danger bit, I'd have been set. My badass reputation assured. As it was, every last one of my brothers—bar Jett—was instructed to keep an eye on me forever more because I couldn't be trusted. That part of the fallout went on years too long as far as I was concerned." He didn't step sideways when everyone else was marching in a straight line for no good reason. "I'm not impetuous," he finished gruffly. "There's always a reason."

"Uh-huh. Baby seals in Alaska."

"I was *six*." Kiss her mouth because it was right there and he couldn't resist. Curl up to a half sit and he could hold that position forever in order to lose himself him her sweetness. "My point is, you can spin a story any way you want, look at a situation from a dozen angles and find both good and bad in it. All you have to do for that foreword is find the right slant and keep the rest of it hidden." He'd moved on from her lips; it was her collarbone that received his attention now. So slender and fine, and from there it was only a short dip to her breasts. So sensitive there as she raked her hand through his hair and directed him where she wanted him. "Yeah?"

"There," she murmured, and he took his time, and savored the freedom with which she gave herself over to him. "And there." He rolled her onto her back, hooked her thigh beneath his arm and slid into her again. It was always like this between them. Unexpected soul baring followed by heart-stopping pleasure, and there was fear in there too for just how much of himself he was giving away to this woman without knowing which way either of them were going.

Thing was, he wanted this. All of it—the good and the bad and all the awkward angles. He wanted her.

And here she was and that was good enough for now.

ROWAN ARRIVED HOME the following afternoon to no fanfare or welcome. Her father had gone to collect Mab from Jock Morgan's and would be back in a couple of days. Beyond that, their ranch foreman and cowboys had everything under control. The house was empty and felt like it and when she walked into her part of it the difference between her living conditions and Casey's couldn't have been clearer. She kept her place neat and clean but it was full of things she'd never bought. Leftovers from another time, her mother's time or maybe her father's parents before that. She'd never known them because they'd had her father late in life, long after they'd given up all hope of ever having a child. In all likelihood they were the ones responsible for the boxy brown leather sofas and wooden tables, wooden floors, whitewashed walls. Not their fault that the place had no color or whimsy or comfort to it.

They hadn't been living in it for the past twenty-four years.

Her kitchen cupboards had never been full of utensils or cookware. Her crockery was beige, thick, heavy and mismatched. She didn't *need* more than four dinner plates.

Casey's kitchen cupboard held matching dinnerware for sixteen and he didn't even live there. For the tourists, he'd said. His mother's doing.

Rowan had sidled past anything to do with mothers.

Her father had never prioritized making living areas super comfortable or pretty. His quarters were sparser than hers. Bare bones and no memories at all.

Tomas James Casey was a bad influence on her. Expanding her horizons with no effort at all. Fine dresses and fancy boots and now she was standing here wanting cushions and throw rugs and laughter and warmth. A dinner set and matching cutlery. Little things, easily affordable, but she'd never wanted them before. Never taken even half a step toward them.

Instead she'd done her damnedest to please her father by staying invisible and working hard. Earning his approval had been her guiding light for as long as she could remember, and she was doing all right in that direction as long as she stayed off the bulls and did her job.

He'd even approved of the bull-riding book and her upcoming week away at the fancy photographer's course. A look of surprise had penetrated the cold and he'd smiled and his eyes had lit up all bright and blue as he'd told her that sounded good, real good. She'd basked in the glow of her father's brief warmth.

Casey didn't do cold. He didn't do closed off. She'd left him with a lingering kiss and a promise to catch up with him in Deadwood and stay on with him after the rest of the tour had moved on. Stay on and make no secret of it, no matter what other people thought.

It was time.

She unpacked and put some washing on, made eggs on toast and opened a bottle of wine that had been sitting cold in the fridge since last year. And then she went to her office, turned on the computer and started looking for cushions and blankets and bed linen and things to put in kitchen cupboards, and vendors who delivered.

Four hours and several thousand dollars poorer, Rowan pushed back from her computer, refilled her wineglass and picked up her phone.

"I'm home," she said. "And I've just been online shopping for household linen and kitchen appliances. I don't even know what some of these kitchen appliances do. But the toaster is purple and it matches the kettle and the wings of the three flying ducks for the wall. I'm also bidding on a wrought-iron chandelier that's approximately the size of a wagon wheel."

"Glad you had a safe trip home," Casey told her.

"That's it? That's all you have to say? I'm blaming your mother's Mad Hatter afternoon tea table and your sixteen-piece dinner set for all of it."

"Did you have fun?"

"Maybe." Maybe yes, once she'd gotten into the swing of it.

"Did you get what you liked?"

"Yes." She was more definite about that.

"So when are you going to invite the family and the foreman and the ranch hands around for a barbecue?"

"What?"

And Tomas James Casey laughed.

Chapter Eight

NINE DAYS, ONE photography course, and many parcel deliveries later, Rowan's first dinner guests arrived at her door, took off their hats and boots, and knocked politely. She'd started small and invited only her father and Mab to dinner. Mab who was still with them while his own father underwent chemo, and who'd somehow wrangled his way into staying in the main house rather than the bunkhouse with the other ranch hands. Rowan had gathered her courage and asked her father why Mab was staying in the house's middle regions and received a sharp stare and a curt 'he's just a kid' for her efforts.

Mab was sixteen.

At *ten* she'd been sleeping in one of the cab cozies in one of the Harper transport trucks while her father had slept in the other. Granted, the trucks had been parked side by side but her father had been noticeably absent on many occasions.

Not that she had anything against lanky, fresh-faced Mab who went out of his way to do things for her. Set the table, take the garbage out, even wage war on the cobwebs on the porch. Right now, Mab was rifling through her fridge for the soda she'd got in especially for him. He was also finding a white wine for her and a beer for her father—Mab the drinks waiter—while her father stood in the middle of her kitchen, his blue eyes baffled and his expression guarded.

He'd held his tongue as the homeware vans and parcels had started coming in. He'd said nothing about the pretty tops and designer sunglasses that had worked their way into her wardrobe or the pretty silk scarf that she'd bought on a whim before deciding it wasn't for her and cutting it up and wrapping it around an old lampshade instead.

Her father studied the bread that had come out of the bread maker minutes earlier and the big red earthenware casserole pot resting on the stove top.

She served the meal on plates of duck-egg blue and, okay, maybe her kitchen was never going to grace the style pages of a glossy magazine but it was progress, and her casserole looked good on blue plates with a sprig of parsley on the top and bread on the side. Not that her father was paying any attention to the food.

He was too busy having a staring competition with the ducks on the wall.

The casserole must have been better than she thought, because her father plowed his way through it, and several slices of the bread, like a starving man. Mab went back for seconds and poured more wine and got her father another beer. Nice boy, always willing to help. Hard to dislike, even when she was looking for things to criticize.

Conversation ranged around bulls and the upcoming weekend in Omaha, and *Hammerfall's* recent shoulder injury and treatment.

Tell a cowboy that the bull who tried to buck them into the sun would stand meekly still while a chiropractor worked on the bull's shoulder with a tennis ball and they'd snort their disbelief, but it was true. Her father didn't keep bulls they couldn't handle, no matter how well they bucked. It wasn't worth the hassle.

The ducks hadn't moved but her father was still keeping an extremely close eye on them.

"More casserole?"

He looked longingly at it, even as he shook his head. "Too full. But it was good. Real good. Your grandma used to make one just like it."

"The recipe was in an old cookbook I found in the attic."

He nodded and shot a furtive glance toward the ducks. Still there.

"I bought them," she said. "The ducks."

"Why?" her father asked.

"Don't you like them?"

"No." Her father always had been decisive.

"I like them," said Mab. "Mallards."

Could be Mab had a teeny-tiny crush on her. Her lack of height and petite frame had never been a help when it came to avoiding the gaze of teenage boys.

"So, next weekend, after Deadwood, I'm staying on to spend the week with T.J. Casey," she said.

Silence.

Could have gone better. "Any questions?"

"Does he have anything to do with the ducks on the wall?" her father asked.

"No, Dad. What is it with the ducks? They're fun. I like them. I bought them. I like Casey too. He's fun. I don't plan on buying him but I do aim to spend more time with him in the future."

"Boy doesn't finish what he starts."

"The *man* had other priorities," she corrected. "He buried his father the weekend of the Vegas finals. He has four brothers and family politics to deal with that you know nothing about." And maybe she shouldn't be speaking of that in front of Mab. Not his business. None of it was. "Anyway. I'll organize one of the hands to cover my work the week after Deadwood. Just letting you know."

Her father stood and reached for his hat. "You don't need my permission to take up with a man, Rowan. You haven't needed it for years."

"Maybe I'd like your blessing."

"I barely know the man."

"You could get to know him. I'm asking you to."

Her father nodded, and then left without saying a word.

Mab stayed behind, looking torn. "I can help you clean up," he offered. Mab, who'd been raised by his mother and who knew his way around a kitchen and had table manners to boot.

"You can if you want." She wouldn't say no to the help. For all that her kitchen now looked the part and she was cooking more regularly than she had been before, she hadn't exactly developed a burning passion for kitchen chores. "How long have you been on the road with your dad now?"

"Since January and the start of the tour."

"Your mom must miss you."

Mab nodded. "She wasn't real happy when my father showed up wanting to take me away for a year. Even less happy when she figured out he was dying. I think she wished he'd never shown up again at all."

"I'd be feeling the same." It was a lot to drop on a sixteen-year-old. "So you chose to come on tour anyway?"

"Wasn't much of a choice. It was now or never if I wanted to get to know him," Mab said bitterly as he reached for the plates and started stacking them. "I call home every week. Ask after what's happening at school and how everyone is, how my basketball team's getting on without their star shooter, see if my dog misses me."

"You could've brought your dog along for the ride."

"It's a miniature poodle."

"Oh." Did he even want to be here, this kid? Or was he simply another displaced child being hauled to and fro? "So are you looking forward to learning how to ride a bucking bull while you're here?"

"Yeah." His lips twisted into a parody of a smile. "No."

OMAHA WAS CHALLENGING in more ways than one. Huck was sitting this one out and so was Paulo, and Casey didn't yet have anyone to stand him in the chute. Someone would—there were always plenty willing—but the familiarity would be missing.

Rowan wasn't here either, and she'd told him she wouldn't be, but there was telling and there was experiencing her absence in full.

He missed standing around the pens with her discussing this bull and that. He missed shouldering up next to her as she watched cowboys ride and the slight lean of her weight into his that said *welcome* and *I'm glad you're here* without her ever having to utter a word.

They hadn't fooled many on the tour with their secret rendezvous or his hot, hard glances in her direction, but at least the other cowboys took care not to rib him when Rowan was around. He'd made it real clear that wasn't on. He was making it real clear to one of the rookies that teasing him about riding worse when Rowan wasn't around wasn't appreciated either, when Joe Harper rocked up and shut that rookie down with one long deadeye stare.

The rookie immediately took his leave. Casey contemplated similar action, but that would be running. So he stayed and waited in silence and watched the latest group of cowboys get set up to ride, while the entertainer entertained and the music blared and a cowgirl in Daisy Dukes and cowboy boots ambled past selling bourbon shooters from a hip belt that also boasted cans of beer, bags of peanuts and empty cups. She had the sales spiel down pat and a smile that promised wholesome fun and she'd been charming the children, flirting with the men and swapping wisecracks with women about the men for near on two hours now.

She was a smart-mouthed tour regular who knew her job and could handle a crowd and she'd taken a pass at Casey earlier, but he'd shut her down gently rather than hard and she was still smiling at him. Rowan's father had most certainly noticed but it couldn't be helped. Those kinds of interactions were part and parcel of being here in the first place.

"Why'd you ride your last bull left-handed?" the older man asked finally, as he too cast his eyes over the action at the chutes. "You didn't need to."

"Practice." True, Casey hadn't exactly turned in a spectacular ride but he'd stuck the eight seconds and the short go was still within reach.

"It's going to cost you. The only bull you need be riding left-handed now is that little dun terror of Rowan's. Unless you're not serious at all about chasing the championship buckle."

"I'm serious." He'd never not been serious about his ambitions, no matter what other people thought.

"They cut you a million-dollar check at the end of the year, what are you going to do with it?"

"Live off it while I go back to college and get the piece of paper that says I have a veterinary degree. Heading back to college is going to happen at the end of the tour whether they cut me that check or not."

The only difference would be in whether he lived easy or hard doing it.

"No more bull riding?"

"This year's my last."

"I've heard that before," said Joe.

"I'm sure you have."

"So if you're leaving, what do you want with my daughter?" The older man had the best poker face Casey had ever seen, and it was a good question. One that had started to come around on repeat.

"Rowan's tied up here, with you and with bull riding." She was, to all practical purposes, bull-riding royalty, even if she didn't see it that way. "I know she's not going to follow me out of the sport, if that's what you mean."

"It wasn't." Joe Harper had a piercing stare. "You could come her way."

Trap.

Say yes and Casey could be accused of gold digging. Say no and he'd be accused of putting his needs and desires before hers.

"I'm ready to finish riding at the end of the season and that's the truth. Riders come and go and so they should. You and all the others like you pick and choose who gets to stay on tour in a different capacity, and we all know I'm not anyone's pick." Never mind Rowan's thoughts on him offering his services as a vet on the tour. That was years away, if at all.

"You could work for me."

Not what he'd been expecting. "Sir, with all due respect because you're the best stock contractor in the business … I don't want to work for you. To be clear, I wouldn't want to work for Rowan either. I don't want to be part of your business or hers. That's not my area of interest. Rowan knows this already. Now you know it too."

Whatever Joe Harper had to say next was interrupted by the next ride. It was one of Harper's bigger bulls, *Hard Landing*, out of the chute and he tossed that cowboy within the first two bucks with a sweet midair roll.

"Beats me why some cowboys ride at all, when nine times out of ten they can't finish what they start," said Joe Harper, his gaze following not the cowboy but the bull as the animal trotted defiantly from the arena. And then the older man turned back to him. "You started something with my daughter, and that's your choice and hers. I hope you have a plan for finishing it without hurting her. I can't see one from where I'm standing, but maybe you're smarter than you look. And like I said: enough with the left-handed showboating. It's not doing you any favors."

The older man walked off. Casey wrapped his hand around the back of his neck, caught the smirk of the nearby cowgirl with the drinks and the hat and figured news of his little chat with Rowan's father would have done the rounds by nightfall.

Casey rode his next bull right-handed, and nailed the ride to pull the best score of the day. He went into the short go in third place, stuck that ride too, and came second overall—losing only to one of the Brazilian competitors who'd ridden solid all the way through.

It didn't escape his notice that Joe Harper had been right about not riding that first bull left-handed. It had cost him the win.

As for this thing with Rowan and how no good was likely to come of it?

Chances were Joe Harper was right about that too.

Chapter Nine

THERE WAS KNOWING something was going to cause you woe … and then there was doing it anyway because it felt so good at the time. Bull riding was like that. Spending time with Rowan was like that too.

The picture-postcard town of Deadwood catered to bikers, tourists, poker players and, every now and again, bull riders. The arena was an outdoor one, small enough for anyone in the crowd to get a real good look at the sport up close. Casey liked that the arena was on the outskirts of the town and that looking out over the stands meant looking up at the black hills beyond. The Deadwood crowd had no need to play at being cowboys and ranching folk because so many of them were exactly that.

Rowan looked like every cowboy's cowgirl dream in this setting. Creamy skin, glossy brown hair that fell where it would, slim-fit jeans, her fancy red boots and that bronzy gold top that screamed money and designer fashion. She had a chute pass, which made her someone, and a camera around her neck, which suggested an occupation. She wasn't officially working this weekend, she'd told him. Her father, Mab and a couple of Harper stock hands had it covered. But she still sat back with him and Paulo and Huck and gave her opinion, and she still shouldered in against him to watch the other cowboys ride.

She was delivering on her promise to make their relationship obvious, and he didn't know how to feel about that. On the one hand it satisfied every instinct he owned.

On the other hand … nope, no complaints … still gut-wrenchingly satisfying.

They had a travel plan for Monday onward that involved Livingstone, Paradise Valley and Marietta, before ending up in Billings for the next stop on the tour. They'd be staying at his cabin for some of that time. He'd made plans to show her around a raptor rehab center.

Until then there was Deadwood and the sweet outdoor arena and the smell of sawdust in the wind and Rowan standing next to him, shoulder to shoulder, leaning in and watching the riders going through the motions.

He'd already ridden once, nothing special but no damage done.

"What do you think of Chase Garrett's chances on *Road To Ruin*?" he asked Rowan as the cowboy in question got ready to ride. Chase had pulled the best bulls all weekend and had ridden *Hammerfall* in the first go for a score of ninety-two. And then a tiny boy had somehow fallen into the arena and the bull had charged and Chase had protected the tike and got trampled for his trouble.

The kid was all right and Chase was riding again and if he stuck the bull Rowan called *Rocky* he'd win the event.

"I like his chances," said Rowan. "I hope he wins."

"Hey! Where's the support?"

"You win enough," she said, and softened her words with a smile. "I'm all for rewarding Chase's bravery."

Hard to argue with that.

Chase's ride was better than good. He stayed on until the horn, and Casey smiled and clapped even as the crowd roared.

"He's done a rib," said Rowan, as Chase walked from the arena. "Look."

It was in the rigid way the cowboy was holding his upper body. All part of the sport.

Casey placed sixth in Deadwood. Nothing to write home about or celebrate, but he couldn't keep the smile off his face afterward and that, beyond anything, was Rowan's doing.

Because she came down to the bar on Sunday night after the event and made good on her promise to claim him, and not in a tacky way. Not by licking his tonsils in public, although he could have worked with that. Not by fawning all over him and hanging off his arm, although he could have worked with that too.

No, she'd done it by the simple act of walking into the bar in fitted jeans, red cowboy boots, another pretty, creamy-colored top and an open jacket and then casting her gaze over the crowd until she found him. And then smiling.

Huck, sitting next to him, had practically snorted his beer. "You are so screwed."

"Huh?"

"That woman *owns* you, man."

"What?" All he'd done was look. "No."

"Plain as day," Huck said sagely. "And stop scowling. Looks like she's heading your way."

THERE WERE MORE terrifying things than walking into a room full of cowboys, their women, and AEBR officials, but Rowan couldn't think of any right this moment. She'd rather face an angry bull than this crowd who watched her every move with an interest born of familiarity, curiosity and sometimes outright malice. Not all the wives who toured regularly with their husbands liked her. She had access to places they couldn't go, an identity that wasn't hitched to any one cowboy, although it could be argued that it was hitched to her father's role and Harper Bucking Bulls.

But her father wasn't here tonight; he was trucking bulls, and she was the Harper representative on the ground. Beyond that she'd told Casey she didn't want to keep their relationship a secret anymore. Come tomorrow morning she'd be spending the entire week with him, heading west rather than south to Wyoming and home. Familiar ground for both of them, familiar enough at any rate, but she'd never traveled those roads as a sightseer before. She'd never gone where the bulls hadn't taken her.

Or tried to claim a man in public.

She had no idea where to even start.

Walking up to him seemed like as good an idea as any, except to do that she had to walk straight past Alicia, who always welcomed her, and Gisele who never failed to do the same. It wouldn't be right to ignore the only women who'd ever made her feel welcome. Maybe they could help her.

Gisele reached out and air-kissed her on both cheeks before drawing back to study Rowan intently. "What's wrong?"

Was it really that obvious? "I told Casey I'd make it clear to everyone I was in a relationship with him this weekend. No more sneaking around."

Alicia smiled. "Aw. How sweet. You seriously think no one's noticed the way you light up—and dress up—just for him?"

"I do not dress up *just* for him!" That would involve sexy underwear—which she may or may not have already purchased with the week ahead in mind. "I'll have you know I wear my new clothes when *no one's* around. Because I like them."

Gisele smirked.

"Anyway … do either of you know how to claim a man in public? Because I'm not quite sure how it's done."

Giselle nodded. "So … are we talking about creating a *drag him from the bar by his belt buckle* moment?"

"Definitely not. And no lap riding either. Or clinging. No clinging."

"Kissing?" asked Giselle. "Somewhere discreet like on his cheek."

"Tempting, but I have tried that in private and my kiss never quite stays on his cheek."

"I'm not surprised given the utter perfection of that man's mouth," murmured Alicia.

Rowan stared at the older woman. "Hey!"

"Catfight," said Gisele sagely. "Always a winner. You wait until some gorgeous thing eases up to him and then drag them away by their hair."

"I'm after something a little less psychotic."

"Good thinking." Alicia signaled the bartender for another champagne. "Listen and learn, younglings. Do you know what he drinks? Top shelf option. Order for yourself and one for him and set his down in front of him."

"What if he keeps right on talking to whoever he's talking to?"

"Honey, he won't—trust me. The man has manners and he'll use them."

"Okay." Rowan was warming to the idea. "So I buy him a drink and sashay on over. Then what?"

"Do you even know how to sashay?" queried Gisele. "Because, frankly, sashaying takes practice."

"She can practice on her way over." Alicia waved away the objection with an expressive hand. "What happens after that is mainly going to involve seating arrangements. Fifty green says he offers you his chair and pulls up another one."

"Or pulls her onto his lap," said Gisele, and Alicia scrunched up her nose and shook her head in a wordless no. "Why not? It happens."

"For all that this is a bar it's still a professional workplace environment where business gets done. Casey's not going to forget that this is Rowan's workplace as well as his. He might put his arm along the back of her chair; I could see that happening. And if someone else makes a move on her or disrespects her all bets are off. But he'll start out polite and respectful."

"I'm sold." Rowan wanted that scenario and she wanted it now. She caught the bartender's eye and he responded with a flirty smile. "Two Pappy Van Winkle Family Reserves please, and make them doubles, and leave the bottle. Room 401." Casey had offered her a glass of the vintage bourbon when they were at his cabin. The very same night she'd promised to acknowledge their relationship when in public.

It didn't get much more public than this.

She signed for the drinks and picked the drinks up in one hand and the bottle in the other and turned to face her women friends. "Wish me luck. And if it all goes wrong you'll come and rescue me, right?"

"Rowan, sweetheart, that's a nine-hundred-dollar bottle of bourbon you're holding," Alicia murmured. "*Everyone's* going to want to rescue you."

"Oh." Who knew? She gave one of the drinks to Gisele and the other to Alicia and asked for two more glasses. "Does this mean I can sashay now?"

"Don't break the bottle," said Gisele. "Go get him."

It went well to begin with. She brushed past Casey's shoulder and set the bottle down in front of him on the table. The glasses came next, empty, but hopefully not for long because she needed something to do with her hands.

Casey stood, his green eyes bemused as he pushed back from the table. "Take a seat. Take my seat while I find another."

"So I'm welcome?"

His eyes flared hot to scorching and her skin felt the lick of it. "Always."

He turned away to find another chair and she slid into the seat and the warmth he'd left behind, and there was dead silence from the cowboys he'd been sitting with, and then as if by unspoken agreement Paulo and Huck on either side of her shuffled their chairs as close as they could get to her, leaving barely an inch of breathing room.

"We're going to need more glasses," said Huck. "What are we celebrating?"

"I'm claiming Casey as mine."

"You should do it more often," said Huck. "Every weekend."

"Let me guess. You're a bourbon guy."

"Mother's milk," said Huck reverently. "Or in this case,

Pappy's milk."

And then Casey was back with a chair that he wedged in between Huck and someone else, and then he put one hand to the back of Rowan's chair and one to the back of Huck's and loomed over them. "Huck, don't make me ask you," he murmured and Huck laughed, even as he moved over one and left the seat next to Rowan free for Casey who settled to it with a sharp grin. "So what are we celebrating?"

"Our sightseeing trip through Montana next week. I'm starting early."

"Because I thought I heard you say you were claiming me," he said as he reached out and uncapped the bottle and poured for her first and then him. "And that's definitely worth celebrating."

"Huck's salivating," she said, but her eyes were for him and the barely leashed want in him. She leaned over and kissed him lightly on the cheek, high up where the temptation to slide right down and find his mouth was lessened and even then she forgot to breathe, pulling away and holding her breath at the fierce promise in his eyes and the way his gaze caressed her lips.

"I'll get water," said Huck. "And more glasses."

"Bring another bottle," said Casey. "We're celebrating."

"Alicia said you'd respect the fact that this is a professional environment for us both."

He was still focused on her lips. "I'm trying. Might help if you stopped looking at me like that."

Rowan smiled crookedly and held his gaze.

"Or that."

It was as close to a whimper as she'd ever heard from this man.

"Sightseeing where?" asked Paulo, and that was a conversation that started with Livingstone and old western films and ended with eagles, and then Huck was back with more glasses and a different bottle of bourbon.

"They didn't *have* another bottle of the good stuff, man," said Huck. "But I'm still the best friend you have here. I gave up my seat for you. And it was all warm and cozy and don't make me beg."

"Huck." Rowan reached for the bottle and gestured toward the empty glasses.

"And she has a generous hand," Huck declared reverently as she poured him a drink and then poured for the rest of the cowboys at the table.

"This is so much better than sashaying over and giving Casey a lap dance," she said, to a chorus of Amens.

"Wait!" spluttered Casey. *"What? Why is it better?"*

"You should drink now," Paulo told Casey with a shit-kicking grin. And then Alicia came over and pulled up a chair, and Gisele and Kit came over too, and all of a sudden it was party time and it was loud and full of laughs and when finally she and Casey left, they left together.

"I claimed you," she said, sliding her fingers through his and tugging him closer as the elevator doors shut and the noise from the bar faded away. "I hope you noticed."

"I noticed."

"Did you like it?" she whispered against the impossible plushness of his lips, right before he kissed her to within an inch of her clothes.

"Believe me," he rasped as the elevator doors opened again and he stepped back to let her out. "I liked it."

THE WEEK THAT followed became crammed with warm smiles and laughter and the hottest sex Rowan had ever known.

Casey showed her his home state and the parts of it he'd fallen in love with as a child. He took her swimming in the hot springs near Yellowstone. They spent a night in Marietta and went to Grey's Saloon for a meal where he filled her in on Jett's bachelor auction and the fallout.

They went to Livingstone and stayed at a historic hotel and went across the road to the open-air cinema one night where John Wayne was playing. He took her to the ice-creamery and the brewery, the chocolate shop and to visit his old mentor at the raptor sanctuary—and she fit.

He took her home to visit his mother and to the cabin again and she loved every moment. There were worlds beyond rough stock transport and bull breeding that she'd never explored and they were open to her.

Some worlds, including the world of hairdressers and beauty products and shopping, fit her regular world far better than she ever thought they would.

Other worlds like the Domestic Goddess world would carry on without her.

Calling Mab's mom the week after the Montana trip and asking her to come and stay for a couple of nights midweek when Mab was here had opened up a whole new world of friendship. Mab's mother wasn't old enough to be her mother but had a whole other world of experience that came with her. *And* she knew bull riding. Didn't like it, mind, but knew it, from a different perspective to the one Rowan knew, and had broken free and ventured beyond it and that was interesting too.

As for what was going on around the Harper ranch, she'd just bought her first rose and dug a hole and half filled it with weathered bull droppings, like the instructions had said. Gardening was new to her too and her association with it might well end up as fleeting as her stint as a domestic goddess. On the other hand, maybe it would stick.

She leaned on her shovel as her father walked up, his face unreadable beneath his cowboy hat.

"You can always ask one of the ranch hands to help with that," he said.

"I know. And if I had fifty of them to plant, believe me I would. But there's only one and I want to do it myself."

"What is it?"

"It's a rose called Renae. It's fragrant. And pink."

Her father nodded as if he cared. "I want to buy you out of the business."

Rowan narrowly avoided falling into the hole she'd dug as she turned to stare uncomprehendingly at her father. "What?"

"The financial advisor says if I take on a silent partner who wouldn't have a majority stake or say in the running of the business, I can afford to buy you out without any loss of running capital."

"But … why?" That was the main question here. "Am I not silent *enough*?"

Her father barely discussed things with her as it was. He ran a tidy, well-resourced operation. Harper Bucking Bulls were well housed, well fed and their breeding program was hands down the most comprehensive in the business. Joe Harper knew the bloodlines he wanted and went after them with ruthless efficiency. He turned over stock transport trucks every three years or one hundred thousand miles, whichever came first. They had a solid ten percent profit margin and didn't owe anything anywhere. On paper, Rowan pulled a wage as a company director. In reality, that money plowed back into the business as needed or sat in a bank account somewhere, accruing interest. She had an expense account to draw from but her recent spending marathon had barely made a dent in it. "Dad, what do you mean? Is this about the ducks?"

Her father snorted. "I want to give you a choice about what you want to do with your life."

And that was just ... another sentence she couldn't comprehend. "You want to give me choice in my life by throwing me out of yours?" Rowan wasn't used to arguing with her father. She was used to keeping her head down and doing what she was told, but not this time. "Dad, what's going on?"

"I talked to that cowboy you wanted me to get to know. I've been watching you both."

"And?"

"He doesn't fit in here."

Rowan blinked. "How do you know? He's never been here." They hadn't crossed that river yet. She wasn't ready for it. She wanted her life to be fuller and prettier before she showed it to him.

"He's not aiming to stick around after the year is out," her father said next, which wasn't exactly news.

"Okay. So? I do know that. But that aside, how do you get from Casey not belonging here to buying me out of the business? That's what I want to know."

"You're doing well with your photographs and—"

"Pictures about bull riding," she interrupted. "Taken while I was on the road with *you*."

"You got accepted into a course."

"I *paid* for that course." Her patience was being stretched. "The book of photos is an interesting project and

I'm invested in making it work, but it's not all I want to do. It's not as if I'm the new Ansel Adams here, Dad. It's a hobby, not a vocation. Besides, who are you going to take on as a silent partner? Who do we know and trust to even do that?"

"Jock Morgan's interested."

"Jock Morgan's *dying*."

"And he has good bull bloodlines and a son he needs to provide for."

Blood rushed from her body, one of those reactions to shock that couldn't be helped, because she could see it now, the way this was shaping. "You want Mab." If she sounded bitter it was only because she was. "You want a son to take over the business one day. God. Doesn't even have to be *your* son, does it?"

"Rowan, listen—"

"If I'd been the son you've always wanted we wouldn't be having this conversation," she snapped. "You'd be proud to build me and hand over to me eventually. Instead you've fought that every step of the way."

"If you were the son I wanted I wouldn't have to factor in you taking off after every two-bit cowboy you fancy yourself in love with!"

Truth. There it was. And it added to the shock and made her colder. "Is this about Casey? It is, isn't it?"

"I've talked to him."

"Oh, yeah? *What did he say?*"

"He doesn't fit in around here, Rowan. He doesn't intend to."

"And Mab *does?*" Hot anger bubbled and overflowed. "Mab barely knows one end of a bull from the other. At the end of the tour he's looking to go back and live with his *mother*. Go to school, play basketball. All those *other* things kids do when they're not loading and hauling bucking bulls from one end of the country to the other!"

"This isn't about Mab, it's about choice." Her father's jaw jutted stubbornly from beneath the hat and shadow concealed his eyes. "The money's there for you to use."

"Use how?"

"However you choose. T.J. Casey's got a direction and he's heading in it. He won't turn around for you."

"And this is news?" She threw the shovel aside and squared up to him, toe to toe even if she barely reached his shoulders. "Since when has anyone ever turned around for me? Have you? Ever? Do you think I'm not fully aware that when it comes down to wants and needs mine come last?"

"*I'm trying to put yours first!*"

Her father, who so rarely raised his voice at either beast or person, was raising it now.

"I'm giving you a way out, with money at your disposal, so you can follow your goddamn cowboy wherever he wants to go. *If that's what you want!*"

She stared at him in silence, openmouthed and dying inside.

"You're nesting," he grated.

"I'm what?" Was she? "What does that even mean? Surely I can have more than one interest in life. I can be more than your shadow and still do my job. You're my family. This is my home and I'm trying to make it how I want it, ducks and roses and all. They'll fit. I'll *make* them fit."

"Rowan, I—"

"No! You don't get to casually toss me aside because I'm no longer needed. This is what I know; it's everything you've taught me and I've worked for it. I don't want to sell my half of the business and take my money elsewhere. And maybe I'm not male, and maybe that matters to some but it doesn't matter to me. I won't be selling and I have *no* plans to take off after Casey."

She took a deep breath.

"If you want to buy Jock Morgan's business when he dies, I'll not say no. If you want to manage it on Mab's behalf and combine the two and bring Mab on board later, I'd consider it—provided he's interested. But I'm going nowhere. You might have built this business and sacrificed plenty but so did I."

She turned her back on him and reached for the rose in the pot. It was big and heavy and as she tipped it on its side to roll it toward the hole her father stepped up to help her.

"I can do it," she grated, and she damn well wasn't talking about the rose. Twenty years on the road. All the politics, all the players and all the crap. Driving until her eyes were ready to fall out of their sockets, one dingy hotel room after the other until the money had started flowing their way. No regular life on her horizon but she'd made do. And now he wanted to take that away from her too. "*Let me do it.*"

"I'm giving you an out," he said quietly.

"I don't want an out. I'm here. I've always been here, whether you've wanted me or not. Deal with it." She had the rose out of the pot and all the roots were showing. The book said to spread the roots out gently and pack soil in around them but to hell with that. She pushed the plant in the hole, picked up the shovel and started packing dirt all around. She'd water it and feed it and it'd survive or it wouldn't. Sometimes life didn't give you the start you wanted but you made do and grew regardless. "Anything else?"

"No. I—no."

He took a step back and then another. She could see several of their ranch hands loitering just inside the barn door … as if standing in shadow meant they were invisible. Her father turned and walked away and she watched him from beneath her cap. She'd always tried to please him no matter what but not this time. She'd fight for the life she had and fight hard.

Just watch her.

Chapter Ten

BILLINGS HAD BEEN and gone. So had Missoula and three between and now it was Tucson's turn to host the AEBR. Right now it was Rowan's job to truck a load of Harper bulls to Arizona. They were only bringing the best of their best this far south. Local contractors could supply the rest, but that still meant eighteen bulls with a combined value of well over seven figures and four transport trucks on the road. Rowan was driving one of them and she was already a couple of hours behind the others. A crazy bladder and sporadic nausea meant she pulled into practically every rest stop on the way. Even the bulls in their individual travel stalls in the trailer knew she wasn't tracking well.

She'd been making good on her promise to herself to create a new life stacked with everything she wanted in it. But there was trying new things on for size and seeing what fit and there was waking up pregnant.

Waking up pregnant wasn't on her to-do list.

Pregnancy came with signs and Rowan had some of them but not all. She was on birth control, but it wasn't infallible.

She had full, oversensitive breasts and needed to pee more often than usual. Both were signs of pregnancy and she'd had them for a while and they'd given her pause.

On the other hand, her menstrual cycles hadn't stopped. Three weeks since the last, and, okay, it had been light. But still present! No pregnancy to worry about.

Right?

The nausea was new and was usually gone by lunchtime. Midafternoon at the most. Another vote for the *you might be pregnant* argument and a compelling one.

Who knew gas stations sold pregnancy test kits?

She bought two test kits and used one and sat in the truck for ten minutes afterward and stared at nothing but blue sky and clouds. She was pregnant, according to the test, and had no idea how far along. Possibly since Cheyenne, ten weeks ago. Possibly a couple of weeks along. She and Casey hadn't exactly been frugal when it came to sex.

It happened every weekend as often as possible.

She had no idea what was going on with her body except that the test said yes and her gut said *I told you so*.

Pregnant, unmarried and Casey, well, Casey had plans that didn't involve her.

At least she had a job, right?

A job she was having trouble doing.

Her phone rang and she looked at the screen. Her father, probably wanting to know where she was. She picked it up and listened to his gruff concern and then spoke.

"Yeah, I've picked up a bug or something. Too many toilet stops. No, it'll be fine. I'll just be slow." She listened some more, to his concerns about getting the bulls where they were going in good order. It was the pointy end of the season and the bulls were traveling as hard as the cowboys, with as much rest built in as possible. "Yes, I'll keep an eye on them. I know it's not ideal, Dad. I'll be there. Yep. Bye."

She sat for ten more minutes fighting nausea and then went to the bathroom again before she started the engine and turned out onto the road. Bulls had to be housed and fed before events and kept in top condition both mentally and physically. Bulls got tired, stressed and burnt out the same way people did, and it was only good management and rest that kept them fresh.

Four more hours on the road and then they could all rest.

ROWAN AVOIDED CASEY on the Friday night before the Tucson weekend. It wasn't difficult. She wasn't staying at the hotel, she was out in a bunkhouse on the ranch the bulls were being held at, and her father was there, and Mab and Jock Morgan too and a couple more ranch hands besides and it was easy to keep up with the pretense that she still wasn't feeling well and wanted to turn in early. She sent Casey a text saying *sorry, not well, no dinner required* and then turned off her phone and the room light, shut the door and crawled into bed.

She'd been working harder than ever since her father had mentioned buying her out of the business. Proving her point, over and over again. Losing weight, not gaining it, and her hand crept to her stomach and the bony jut of her hips. How on earth could there be a baby in there? She could barely believe it.

She hadn't been eating well, hadn't been taking good care of herself let alone another. As for being a mother, her own mother had died in childbirth and wasn't *that* a cheerful thought to take to sleep.

The test might have been wrong.

There might *be* something wrong. With her. With the pregnancy. A positive test and bleeding still. What was going on there?

At two in the morning Rowan got up and took the second pregnancy test to the bathroom with her.

This one was positive too, and either they were both wrong or she was well and truly screwed.

Around four a.m. she drifted into a restless sleep and at a ten to six her father banged on her door.

"Rise and shine," he boomed, and thundered on Mab's door too—this was equal opportunity torture. But she got up and showered and checked her phone for the draw for the weekend to see which cowboy was riding which bull. Casey had drawn two good Harper bulls in the prelim rounds, which should work to his advantage. *Hammerfall*, *Eggs* and *Rocky* were being held for the final round—no surprises there.

She headed out into the common bunkhouse area and found her father and Jock already all over the draw and thought wistfully of the bed she'd left, thin and meager as it was. She took her own pillow and bedding with her these days—years of travel and rough sleeping had taught her the benefits of that and she'd passed her expertise to Mab, going so far as to take Mab shopping for the basics. Pillow, sheets and fluffy blankets had been her staples.

Mab's version of comfort varied somewhat in that he'd make do with a sleeping bag, but his mother had sent him his pillow from home.

An ordinary pillow, lumpy and old.

From home.

Nausea hit hard as Mab handed her a plate full of pancakes and bacon, but she thanked him and took the plate outside and sat at the tiny table for two on the porch. Minutes later Mab set a cup of tea by her side, black and hot, and dumped a handful of sugar sachets beside it.

"How are you feeling?" he asked.

"Fine."

"Cause you look like shit."

"Yay." Good thing this place was blessedly free of mirrors.

"I can cover for you today if you want," offered Mab the

ever helpful. He was impossible to dislike, and she wanted to dislike him quite a lot.

She reached for a sugar.

"I've already put two in and stirred. That's how you take it, right?"

"Right." Utterly impossible to dislike, no matter how much others favored him over her. "Thanks." She put the sugar down and reached for the tea, and it was weak and sweet and perfect. She took another tiny sip because slowly-slowly said her stomach. "I'll let you know if I need help." Mab was a good kid. Always willing to pitch in and surprisingly observant. Wasn't his fault she was jealous of him.

Wasn't his fault she was pregnant.

"There is something you can do for me right now." She pushed her breakfast plate toward him. "It looks wonderful, but I can't eat it."

"You didn't eat last night either."

"Stomach bug. I've been fighting outright food revolt since yesterday, but thanks for the tea. The tea is good." The tea was great. She could even keep it down.

Bonus.

Mab retreated with the food and she closed her eyes and leaned her head against the weatherboard wall. The bulls didn't need to be at the arena until midafternoon. Rise and shine was all well and good but they only had a quarter of the bulls here that they usually had and surely they had enough hands here to see to them without adding hers.

On the other hand, someone usually checked in at the arena early to make sure everything was ready for them when they arrived—and that someone was usually her. She didn't want to be here beneath her father's watchful gaze, or anyone's gaze. Not really.

Find Casey. Confess. Watch him whoop for joy.

Yeah, she couldn't picture that either.

Find Casey, confess, and watch his respect for her fade and the joy they'd found in each other crumble?

Far more likely.

THERE WAS ONE fatal flaw in Rowan's cunning plan to curl up somewhere at the arena and wait for her nausea to pass and that was that people here knew her habits and took note of unexpected behavior.

Apparently sitting in the stands with her knees up and her cap covering her face was enough to stop Troy Jensen in his tracks.

"Rowan?"

She pushed the brim of her cap up and stifled a sigh. "Hey, stranger. Good to see you back." Troy had been riding in the lower grades for part of the season and had clawed his way back up.

"Good to be back," he said and she smiled. She liked the suntanned Aussie, even if his reputation for playing fast and loose with women was utterly deserved.

"Casey about?" Troy asked next, and that was most unfair. Troy had been back on the circuit for approximately five minutes and already he knew that she and Casey were a thing?

"We're not joined at the hip."

If Casey had any sense he'd still be in bed. She hadn't turned her phone on to see if he'd left any messages. Her current train of thought was imbecilic in the extreme but ran something along the lines of if Casey didn't exist maybe her pregnancy wouldn't exist either. "I'm waiting for a couple of the powers-that-be to get out of bed so I can talk bull business with them," she offered. "You?"

"Just got in," he said. "Coffee?"

He had coffee in hand and he held it toward her and in some other universe she might have applauded his generosity. As it was her stomach reeled, even as she sat up fast and put her hand out to turn it away.

"Guess not," he murmured.

"I've gone off coffee," she said weakly.

"Right." He eyed her warily, and then seemed to come to some kind of a conclusion. "Don't go anywhere."

He headed back the way he'd come, one shoulder hitched slightly higher than the other, and returned minutes later with a cola in hand and no coffee in sight. "Try this."

It was cold, crisp and perfect. She didn't guzzle it but she definitely wasn't giving it back.

"Only thing my mother could keep down some mornings," he said and there was an undercurrent of something in his voice that she couldn't quite place. "Just remember there's bugger all nutrition in that crap. It doesn't replace good calories and if the pain persists see your doctor," he said with a twist of his lips.

"Okay," she said. "Thank you. You feeling good about being back?"

He smiled all slow and lazy and there was a world of words behind a smile like that but he didn't offer any and she didn't push. "Take care of yourself, Rowan. Yell if you need a hand."

Bemused, she watched him swagger away. Troy had never offered to help her do her job before. The bull riders left the handling of the bulls to the people who owned them—this was a hard and fast AEBR tour rule, and breaking that rule had consequences. Was she oozing *help me I'm pregnant* pheromones she didn't know about?

Because she could have sworn that man had taken one long look at her and *knew*.

AVOIDING CASEY LATER in the day was easy provided Rowan stayed busy. He rarely interrupted her when she was working, and she made sure to sidle up and say hello and lean into his shoulder as she traded greetings with Paulo. Nothing to see here, nothing wrong. The man had bulls to ride and winning to concentrate on. He'd risen to third place in the standings overall—a combination of several wins and solid riding all the way through. He was on track for Vegas and taking enough prize money to see him through the study he wanted to do, and after that, who knew?

She doubted babies featured in his plans anytime soon.

She didn't know how to tell him. She'd barely come to terms with it herself other than there would have to be changes made when it came to her work and that her father was going to want to get rid of her even more now. She tried not to dwell on it as she swung up behind chute four and got ready to tie the flank strap on the Harper bull Paulo had drawn.

Casey was in place to help Paulo get set to ride, nothing unusual about that, and then two bulls later Paulo would be doing the same for Casey. Those two had a no-nonsense, lightning-fast chute system in place and Rowan was happy to play her part. They both liked the flank strap tightened later rather than earlier, preferably as they finished securing their hand. A nod from her toward whoever was standing the bull and he'd pat the rider on the vest and remove his hand and then it was up to the rider when to go.

As a system it was one of the fastest on the circuit, adrenaline rich and effective, requiring split-second timing from all players involved, and Rowan was happy to play her part.

This bull bucked better when the flank strap was further

forward than usual, which meant setting it in place beneath and then climbing the rail and leaning over to work it into place on the bull's back. She'd done it a million times before, but never while dizzy, never when her vision was a rapidly closing tunnel.

She waited, counting off the seconds while Paulo got his bull rope in place and Casey pulled it tight and waited for Paulo to resin up before handing the rope back for the wrap. She could see parts of the process on a normal day given that she was behind them both but she could see barely any of it today with the tunnel vision.

She took her cue from the way they moved rather than the little things, and tightened the flank strap and tied off on it by memory rather than vision. Her small size meant that she hooked one leg over the rail to do her job and set her back foot on the rail second from the top. It was a secure position, well out of harm's way, only today not so much as she swayed forward and then there was an arm like a band around her waist and she looked back and it was Troy.

Troy with the coffee and the cola and the all-seeing eyes.

"You right?" he asked, and Casey was looking at them and she nodded and gave Casey the thumbs-up. He thumped Paulo's vest once and took his hand away, and Paulo nodded and was gone like clockwork.

At least she hadn't stuffed that up, except that she was sagging against Troy and still balanced precariously on the rail and the world was spinning too damn fast for her to catch hold of.

"Let go of the rail," Troy murmured. "I've got you."

Hell, no. That rail was the only thing that wasn't pitching forward.

"Casey, come get her," Troy said next, but Casey was already there and maybe she could let go now, and she was tilting sideways and smacking her head against his chest and clutching at his arms. They were warmer and larger than the railing and she couldn't get her hands around his biceps, so she tried to fist her hands in his shirt but that wasn't working either because he was wearing his vest and that sucker was clench proof and horn proof and made out of new-age ballistic material. The hell with Kevlar. Kevlar was old.

"I'm all right," she said. Where was the floor? It was metal and shaped like little leaves but it was solid enough. "Let me sit awhile."

"Yeah, not here," he said, and she closed her eyes and pressed her cheek to his vest and breathed his familiar scent and let go. He was there. And that was all.

Chapter Eleven

CASEY PACED THE wide corridor outside the sports medicine room. He'd never been more grateful to have a medical team on site, but they weren't letting him in the room in and Rowan had been in there for fifteen minutes. He was quietly going out of his mind.

Paulo had caught up with him after the ride but had left five minutes later saying he was going to try and get Casey's ride time changed to the next round. Casey didn't like the other man's chances of winning any concessions in that regard but it beat Paulo standing around and watching him come undone.

What was wrong with her? Why was no one saying anything?

Rowan had passed out in the chutes and hadn't come to until he'd laid her out on the stretcher in that room and she'd been so light and pale in his arms. Too light and fragile and those eyes so full of warmth and light had been closed and her body boneless.

She'd seen him and let go of the rail, reached out toward him, her eyes wide and frightened, and what the hell was wrong with her?

Because Doc Freeman had ordered Casey from the room and shut the door in his face, and what was that all about? Since when had the doc demanded privacy when treating patients?

Granted, Rowan was a woman. Maybe that was it.

And patient confidentiality.

And the fact that Casey wasn't next of kin.

Where the hell was Rowan's father in all of this? Because if he was next of kin he should be here, in there, finding out what was wrong so that Casey could stop pacing.

Someone else appeared in the tunnel, a dark silhouette against the bright light, cowboy hat on, but it was only Paulo and that was all he needed—a reminder of the wider world and his obligations to it. He had a bull to ride, and no leeway whatsoever when it came to not getting out there and doing it.

"They'll hold your ride 'til the end of the round," Paulo said when he reached him. "Which means you've got ten minutes to get back to the chute. Mab says Rowan's been off with a stomach bug for a couple of days and hasn't eaten much. Troy said much the same, with one minor point of difference." Paulo looked to the door. "You should ride."

"Not until I see her."

"She's in good hands," Paulo persisted. "Management's being as understanding as they're gonna get. You need to ride."

"Not until I find out what's going on."

The door opened and the doc peered out. "You're still here?" he said.

Casey didn't take his eyes off the older man's face. "How is she?"

"She fainted. Low blood pressure."

"*Now* will you ride?" asked Paulo.

"Can I see her?"

Paulo put his hand on Casey's forearm. "Are you deliberately trying to kill your career?"

"I'm *trying* to find out what's wrong with Rowan."

"Casey." Rowan was in the doorway, wan but upright.

He was in her space in an instant but he didn't know where to touch. She was standing. She wouldn't be doing that if there was anything drastically wrong. He took that thought and held to it. "What happened? And why are you standing?" He glared at the doc. "Why is she standing?"

"Good question, seeing as I told her to stay put until we got some food into her."

"Well, I might have stayed put if some cowboy I know wasn't intent on ruining his career." She took his hand and hers was warm and moving. "I fainted. It happens. Get out of here. Don't you dare put me before you. Not for this. I'm okay, so please, Casey. Go. I've got this."

He searched her face, still pale, but her eyes were clear and filling with tears as he gathered her close, peppered her with soft kisses to the edge of her brow and the curve of her cheek. "You scared me stupid."

"Go." She pushed out of his arms and leaned against the wall. "Please don't screw up because of me."

But still Casey hesitated. It didn't feel right to go when every bone in his body wanted to stay. "You're sure you're okay?"

"I'm okay."

"Go." Doc Freeman's voice was firm but not unkind. "We've got this."

FIVE MINUTES LATER he was in the chute and he'd never been more grateful for the professionals at his side, although seeing Joe Harper acting as flank man caused a hot lick of anger in him, especially seeing as the older man didn't even ask how his daughter was. "Why didn't you come to the medical room?"

"Someone had to be here to pick up Rowan's slack."

"She's not slack, she's *sick*. She works herself to the bone for you and you treat her like an inconvenience. You don't even ask how she is."

"Maybe if you rode your fucking bull the way everyone's waiting for you to, I can finish my job and go and find out."

And then Paulo was wedging his way between them and pushing on Casey with not inconsiderable strength. "Ride the bull, amigo. You don't want to do this."

"Oh, but I do."

"Yeah? And what happens when your girl finds out you've screwed her father over as well as yourself? Think she'll be happy about that?"

Fuck.

Save it for the ride, my friend.

It was the fastest setup in history. Eight seconds later he was still on his bull and the siren sounded and he put his free hand to his bull rope and started looking for an exit.

He scored high, a ninety, and figured it for a gift because his attention had been anywhere but on the ride or the bull beneath him. He'd just wanted it done.

He climbed back over the chutes, blood pumping, adrenaline coursing, and he *knew* now wasn't the time to confront Rowan's father. Didn't even look around for him, just packed his mouth guard away, rolled up his bull rope and grimly set about thanking the riders who'd shuffled forward to allow him to ride last.

He did have manners, see? He wasn't all about hot temper and raw words and being right.

See to his gear, walk back to his truck. Cool down some before he went looking for invalid soup or at least something that had more nutrition to it than a donut. Let Rowan's father have some time with her, if indeed that was where the man had disappeared to.

It was a good ride and he was in the lead again and that meant riding tomorrow and having his pick of the bulls for the short go, and it'd probably be a Harper bull he chose, and *fuck*. Meanwhile he had to find chicken soup and get it delivered and take Rowan to his room and tie her down and make her rest until she was better—

"You realize you're talking aloud."

Casey turned to find Huck watching him from the other side of a bull pen. "What?"

"Chicken soup, rest, tying her down."

Ah.

"Sounds like a plan," Huck said. "Whereas pissing all over Papa Harper was a terrible plan. He'd already phoned the doc from the back of the pens and whatever the doc told him was enough to keep him where he was and doing his job."

Casey wiped his hands over his face.

"I'm guessing you didn't know that," said Huck.

"They threw me out of the treatment room. I didn't know what was going on. I still don't." People didn't faint when there was nothing wrong with them, but then, she'd told him she had a stomach bug last night when she bailed on him and he'd barely seen her since. Stomach bug. No food. Physical work. Fainting. It made sense. "Maybe I over-reacted."

"You think?"

Not a question that needed any kind of answer.

"You're gone on her, man. All the way, shut the gate."

"Yeah, well, thank you, Einstein." He'd come to the

same conclusion on the twenty-year walk from the chutes to the medical rooms with an unconscious Rowan in his arms. He'd looked down at her as he'd laid her on the stretcher bed and she'd been the beginning and the end for him and everything in between, and he'd been plea-bargaining with God for her to wake up and be okay, and now he needed to lean his elbows on the fence rail and stick the heels of his hands to his eyes and breathe and be and know that she was still there with him. "How do you stand it?"

"Stand what?" Huck was still there, a solid, steady presence.

"Love."

Huck huffed a laugh. "Wait 'til you have kids."

"I'm not having kids." Not if it felt like this. "Never been part of the plan."

And then Huck turned and kicked Casey's foot, straightened and cleared his throat. "Hey, Rowan. How you feeling?"

"I've been better."

Casey stood and turned and wondered how much of the conversation she'd heard.

"I hear you rode well," she said with the ghost of a smile, and her father was right there beside her, a tense and silent presence.

"You're even whiter than you were before," he muttered. "Why aren't you lying down?"

Big brown eyes in a starkly pale face looked back at him

and she let out a ragged breath and then a laugh that sounded more like a sob. "I will be soon. I came to say I'm heading home for a while. Wanted to tell you so in person."

"Home as in Wyoming?" Because they were a solid twelve hundred miles away from Wyoming. "You're driving?"

"Flying."

"And who's flying with you?"

"Mab," she said.

Morgan's kid, and that was okay in as far as it was someone, but it wasn't him. "I'll do it."

"You have bulls to ride," she said, and stepped up and wrapped her arms around him and held him close. His arms went around her, they always would, but there was something off about this embrace and he didn't know what. Her father was staring out over the arena as if giving them privacy, even if not space, and Huck had his head down and was scuffing the ground with his boot.

"I'll come as soon as I can." He spoke into her hair because her cheek was to his chest.

"No, it's okay." She pulled back, out of his arms, her eyes searching his face as if memorizing him. "Go get those points, cowboy."

Something was wrong. "Why did you faint?"

"I wasn't looking after myself. It won't happen again." She stepped away from him and her father both, slight of form as she turned away, head down and shoulders hunched.

Her father made to leave only Casey had something to say.

"Got a minute? Sir?"

"Sir now, is it?" And yeah, there was Huck melting away, catching up with Rowan and walking with her toward the Harper trucks.

Casey squared his shoulders and turned his attention back to the other man and prepared to take his licks. "I'm sorry for what I said back there. I shouldn't have said it. I was out of line."

"Maybe you were. Maybe you weren't." Joe speared him with a glance. "I lost my wife and son because I failed to protect. You'd think I'd have learned my lesson by now but I still make bad choices. I give Rowan too much rope or too little. I put work first because it's right there in front of me and it's easier than thinking something might be wrong. You don't do that. You put my daughter first and I respect that. She deserves that. So keep doing it."

"I KNOW WHAT'S wrong with you. I'm not stupid," said Mab three days after they arrived back at the ranch. It was midafternoon and they were sitting on the porch. Mab had put together a snack of fresh fruits and yogurt that he'd driven all the way into town to buy. Rowan had been thoroughly appreciative as they'd sat down to eat, but at his quietly challenging words the flavorsome berries turned to dust in her mouth.

"You sent your coffee machine down to the bunkhouse and all the beans with it because you can't stand the smell of coffee anymore. You can't keep food down of a morning and you've swapped out tea for clear soup. Can't keep that down half the time either and yesterday you drove to the hospital in Casper. They phoned to remind you of your appointment after you'd left." Mab had a stubborn jaw. She'd never noticed it before. "You're pregnant."

Three months pregnant and counting, underweight and tired enough to want to sleep sixteen hours a day. The specialist had been all for it. Get some rest, build your strength. See me in a week and don't make me admit you.

The fear was constant, and it wasn't just because she already wanted this baby with all of her heart, never mind that Casey didn't. Casey didn't know, didn't *have* to know right now. Might never need to know if things didn't work out.

"You could talk to my mom," Mab said doggedly in the face of her continued silence. "She's a good listener and she'd know stuff. All kinds of stuff like how to get through this part and how to cope later on when the father's not around. I turned out all right, didn't I?"

Rowan had to put her spoon down and look away and wipe at a tear that had swollen at this man-child's earnestness. "I'd be well pleased if any kid of mine grew up as kind as you."

"I could ask her to come," he said. "You could ask her to

come. You asked before."

"To see *you*." And even then, Rowan had no real idea if the woman had been able to afford the airfares involved or the time away from her job. "Your mother works."

"She'd come if I asked. If I thought she was needed here."

"It's a nice thought." It really was. "But this isn't your mother's problem. I can't ask her to drop everything and come running because I'm—" She couldn't even say it out loud for fear of jinxing herself and losing her baby five minutes after acknowledgment.

"No," he said agreeably, but why was he nodding yes? "But I can."

HER FATHER ARRIVED home on Monday the following week. Rowan hadn't been expecting him, and he certainly hadn't been expecting to see Mab's mother making herself comfortable in Rowan's kitchen, making chicken soup while Rowan sat at the table with the computer on and a spreadsheet open, calculating the increased wage costs of having one of the ranch hands take her place on the circuit. She could afford to employ someone in her own right if her father objected.

Her father was taking his hat off and standing at the door as if unsure of his welcome.

"Lenore," he said to Mab's mother.

"Joe."

"Surprised to see you here."

"You're halfway to stealing my son out from under my nose," Lenore countered. "It seems only fair I get a daughter in return."

"Mab's here because Jock's having more chemo," her father said.

"I know where Jock is," said Lenore coolly. "I know what it's doing to my son. I might even thank you one day for taking Mab under your wing the way you have, but it won't be today. Tea?"

"Coffee if you have it."

"Coffee machine's down at the bunkhouse," said Rowan. "Help yourself."

"Tea's fine. Black, strong, no sugar." Her father's gaze shifted to the living breathing lump of tight curls and liquid brown eyes at Rowan's feet. "What's that?"

Truly, who wouldn't crack a smile? "It's a poodle."

"And why is it here?"

"It's Mab's poodle. It came with Lenore."

"And Lenore is here why?"

"Because we needed her." Rowan had never seen her father quite so wary of a woman before. It would have been amusing had she not been so instantly wound up about telling him things he needed to know. "Take a seat, Dad. How did you get here?"

"Flew and then hired a car."

"Why?"

"You tell me."

Lenore set a pot of tea and an empty mug on the table. "I'll see to the washing on the line."

She left and her father sat there, making no move toward either teapot or mug. "Rowan, what's going on? You text me last night to say you're not finishing out the tour and sending someone else along in your stead and then you won't take my calls."

"Because it was eleven p.m. and I went to bed. I called you back this morning and you didn't pick up."

"Because I was in the air."

"I'm three and a half months pregnant."

Nothing. Not even the tick of a jaw.

"And I'm failing to thrive. Me and the baby both."

He pushed back, out of the chair and was out the door without a word. She followed at a slower pace and Mab's poodle went with her. She got as far as the screen door and couldn't open it when she saw her father crouching at the bottom of the steps with his hands in his hair and his head bowed, his elbows braced for a blow. She saw Lenore with the washing basket walk up and put her hand on his shoulder, before taking his hand and drawing him up and into her arms.

Comfort and he took it, her proud, taciturn father who'd never wept, not once, but his shoulders were shaking and his head was low. Rowan wrapped her arms around her waist

protectively and leaned against the wall and closed her eyes.
　　One down.
　　One to go.

Chapter Twelve

GETTING CASEY TO visit was easier than she'd thought it would be. All she had to do was phone and ask. He'd booked his flight before he'd got off the phone, and arranged to arrive the following day around midday, travel willing. Rowan told everyone at dinner that he was coming and Lenore, lovely Lenore who'd talked and coaxed and told Rowan her own life story and who Rowan had nothing but respect for … Lenore said she and Mab were heading into town for supplies. Her father, unasked, said he had things to do in town too so he'd drive them. It meant privacy and one less worry in the form of confrontation between Casey and her father and for that Rowan was grateful.

"How are you going to tell him?" Lenore asked as she passed the potatoes, and Rowan laughed a little because this was the level of openness Lenore and Mab had brought to her life and she cherished it and craved more.

"I'm open to suggestions."

"Don't start by telling him you're off to a rough start," her father offered gruffly. "That one's a kicker."

"I won't." Lesson learned.

Her father had since revealed her mother's pregnancy histories. The rough first trimesters and the settling in the second and the blossoming in the third. Her mother had bled out. A torn placenta close to term and medical help too far away. Her father had kept all the medical records; they'd been filed under N for no and he'd brought them out and talked and *talked*. Rowan had learned more about her mother in one night than she had in twenty-four years, her strong and silent father splitting himself open the better for them to mine any bit of information that could be of use, and it had hurt him but he'd done it.

For Rowan and the baby in her womb.

"How did you tell Jock?" Rowan asked Lenore.

"You don't want to do it that way either," said Lenore dryly.

"You tell Casey how you feel about him first. That's what I'd want," Mab said quietly. "'Cause there are two issues to think about here. Whether you love him. And how you feel about having his baby. Then whether you want to be a family. That's three things," Mab amended.

"That's my boy." Lenore's smile was soft and proud.

"Aaw, you made your mama cry," Rowan teased, and Mab shot his mother a startled glance.

"Mom, don't. Stop." He looked helplessly toward her father. "*Why?*"

"So what does Mab stand for?" asked Rowan between smiles.

"Macallister Ahtunowhiho Beowulf Morgan," said Lenore with relish.

Mab blushed beetroot red. "Again with the *why*?"

"Family names, all of them, and all of them beautiful." Lenore smiled unrepentantly.

"They're going in the naming box," said Rowan. "All of them and Lenore too." Because they'd both made this so much easier than it could have been.

"Casey's been hauled over the coals again for not being committed to the tour," her father said. "He won't be riding next year, even if he wants to."

"But, what?" She'd heard nothing. "Why? Did *you* have anything to do with this?"

"No, but you did. He nearly missed his ride, taking care of you. If you hadn't been okay he wouldn't have ridden at all. They say he's too distractible."

"Shows what they know," said Lenore scathingly. "Where are their family values now?"

"He also got fined for an incident involving me and him at the chute before a ride."

"No wonder you want to come into town with us," said Lenore. "But keep going. Confession is good for the soul. What else do we need to know?"

"I argued against both the fine and the ruling for next year."

"Would you like applause?" said Lenore, but her father ignored her and focused on Rowan.

"He can be a vet anywhere once he finishes his studies. Even here. Start his own business, be his own man, but do it here. With you. What I'm trying to say is give him a chance and plenty of options to be going on with. He might be shocked speechless, he might not. It's a lot to take in, but I know what I saw on his face when he carried you off. It was terror. Nothing but you and only you, the end of his world right there in his arms. And I do know how that feels."

CASEY TURNED OFF the road and drove beneath the ironwork arch declaring the ranch Harper Bucking Bulls. He was in Northern Wyoming and already calculating the distances from this place to Montana. Not as far as he'd thought. Not that far away and maybe …

His world was full of maybes these days and one of those maybes involved the reason behind Rowan's continued absence from the tour. Mab was gone too. Joe Harper had returned home and that was the clincher.

If Rowan hadn't phoned and invited him to come he'd have hightailed it here regardless, because something was wrong and maybe, just maybe, it had to do with fainting and lack of appetite and a reason for that that didn't involve a stomach bug.

No one was saying she was pregnant, not in front of him, but it was on his mind and the minds of others, and if she was … God. If she was pregnant, the last she'd seen of him was him swearing off children forever.

And that was all kinds of wrong.

Fear had driven that statement. His total inability to absorb what he'd been feeling and handle it rationally rather than with a gut response for it to stop.

He'd do whatever she wanted, whatever it took in order for him to remain a part of her life. More riding, although he'd screwed that well and good. Another tour. A different tour. No tour at all and a job here in Wyoming. Get sponsored to finish his education in pieces. Give him a chance and he'd sort it, and the Harper ranch was quality acreage, no doubt about it. No wonder she was invested. He would be too if this was half his and likely to be all his one day. A family legacy, built and paid for by years of hard toil and sacrifice. He didn't have to be part of it, but he sure as hell wanted the chance to work around it.

The barn was a mansion. The main house was almost as big. Both were orderly and somewhat bare around the edges. There was no whimsy here. He parked out front of the house and headed left, as directed. Rowan's quarters were to the left of the main double doors. Walk the porch, go around the corner—this was her part of the world.

A tiny, mostly bare rose had been planted in the middle of the grass lawn that ran this side of the house, the earth still bare around it. So new it hurt to look at, because his mother planted roses, one for every family pet that died, and if that was a death rose what was beneath it? Rowan had never spoken of pets.

Rowan had never spoken about a lot of things.

His footsteps were loud as he walked the planks of the porch and stopped at the door that another set of steps led up to. He knocked, loud in the silence, but the beating of his heart seemed louder still.

She came to the door and opened it, and one of his concerns fell like a weight from his shoulders because Rowan was standing; Rowan looked well, good color in her cheeks and a smile on her lips.

"You made it," she said, and there was a lot going on in her eyes. Hesitation. Shyness. Fear. And welcome.

"Your directions were good." He leaned down to kiss her, lips, no hands, so she could pull away if that was what she wanted, only she didn't pull away. She opened to him, sweet as nectar, and he needed no second invitation as he deepened the kiss and got lost.

"You missed me," she said, when finally she pulled back. He still hadn't touched her anywhere else, and his body near vibrated with the effort of holding back.

"So much."

She was hovering halfway between inside and out.

"May I come in?"

"Can we—" She hesitated and her gaze slid past him to the view of the barn and the rolling hills and the higher ones on the horizon. "Can we sit on the steps and talk first?"

So he sat with her on the steps and stared at the rose and something was coming but he didn't know what.

She sat close enough for their shoulders to brush, so she wasn't against his touch, but her eyes were on the horizon and her hands were clasped around her knees and her knuckles were white.

Small hands but there was strength in them—and sinew.

"So this is my home, and I'm beginning to appreciate it more and more," she began. "What it could be if someone decided to stay here and love it the way it should be loved. I have you to thank for that, or maybe your mother and Mab's mother too. She's been staying here and doing things. Fixing things up the way I've never thought to, but that's not what I wanted to talk about, not really. It's only part of it. I'm not rejoining the tour. I'm done with it."

"Why?"

"Long time coming?" she replied with a lilt to her voice that made it a question. "But that's not where I wanted to start. Can we start again?"

He looked at the rose and the freshly dug earth and swallowed. "Sure."

"I love you. You should know that straight up. I fell in love with you that first morning at breakfast when I bolted my food and you pushed yours aside, half finished, and asked if I was ready to go shopping."

"I fell in love with you when you scolded a bad-tempered bull as if it were a piddly puppy and then proceeded to feed him slices of pumpkin from your pocket. Wasn't a puppy, Ro." Casey smiled at the memory. "I fell in love with you even more when some supermodel type criticized your working-woman hands and you shoved them in your pocket and walked away. I wanted to follow." He took a deep breath and turned to look at her profile. "I had a quiet yet raging epiphany when you fainted on me. I'd follow you anywhere."

"I'm pregnant."

He closed his eyes, awash with relief. No loss buried beneath that bare little rose. "Good."

She sagged against him, her bony shoulder digging into his arm, and it was familiar enough to be comforting but if he reached for her now he wouldn't get to say what he needed to say and they had to talk.

"You told Huck you didn't want kids."

"That was fear talking. Cowardice. I can't imagine feeling more vulnerable about children than I feel about you. It's too big already. I couldn't even imagine it. That depth of love."

"I'm drowning too," she murmured. "Want to go down together?"

"Yes."

"I'll come with you if you want me," she said next. "To Davis, California, while you finish your studies. To Washington State. I want us to be together, but after that I want us to be here. I want to raise my family here, not on the road. I want to build my life here. With you. You could build your practice here. Arrange things so Harper Bucking Bulls doesn't swallow you whole."

"I can do that."

"There's more."

How could there possibly be more?

"Mab and his mother are shifting here too. She's a bookkeeper. She's going to be keeping our accounts, going forward. We're combining stock operations with Jock Morgan and taking on a third business partner."

"Mab?"

"Mab's mother, until he's old enough. They're good people. And Jock won't be around to look after them. My father gets the son he's always wanted and I get to pull back and concentrate on taking care of myself. Because there's more."

Dear Lord.

"It's a high-risk pregnancy. I'm small and underweight and can barely keep anything down but it's getting better. I'm resting a lot and taking good care." Her hand crept into his and he squeezed and brought it to his lips and vowed not to fall apart in front of her.

"Okay." Her hands weren't soft like some. They were calloused, same as his. "But if it comes to a choice you should know I'll always choose you. Write it on your heart, because it's written on mine."

"College boy with the fancy phrases," she whispered.

He could say plain words too. "I love you."

"I love you too."

"Will you marry me?" He wasn't on his knees but she wasn't standing up either.

"When?"

"Soon." As soon as possible. "Vegas." End of the tour, beginning of a whole new world.

"What if you don't win there?" He'd get there; they both knew that. "You'll be cross."

"No I won't. I'll be with you." Now he could reach for her, pull her into his lap and hold her and never let her go. "I've already won."

"Then yes," she whispered against his lips. "I'll marry you."

Epilogue

THE HOSPITAL WAITING room was crammed full of cowboy boots and many hats and men enough to fill them. Rugged types, built strong, and those would be Casey's brothers. Leaner types, more wiry but no less powerful and those would be the bull riders. That was what Rowan told the midwife in between the waiting to push and the panting.

She'd almost made it to full term with her pregnancy, only a couple of weeks shy of it and that was good because the baby was still small enough for an easy birth. The tour had been in Washington State that weekend, where Casey was finishing his studies, and Paulo and Huck had been visiting when she'd gone into labor. Good thing too, because Casey had panicked and her father had panicked and it was eighteen hours later and chances were they were still panicking.

Could be she'd called this labor a little too early. How was she to know?

But the midwife was smiley and reassuring and kept going out to the waiting room and returning with reports.

"Who's the older one who hasn't stopped pacing since he got here? The one with the blue eyes and the thousand-yard stare?" asked the midwife as she took Rowan's hand in hers and studied the readouts on the machines.

"That would be my father."

"And the woman who waltzed in and sat him down and made him drink tea with sugar in it?"

"Mab's mother, Lenore," Rowan grated and then a contraction got her in a vise-like grip and made her roar. "When can I push?"

"Soon. You're almost there."

"She was almost there *two hours ago*." This from Casey who held her other hand and could have used a tea with two sugars as well, or at least a dose of Lenore.

She'd ask them all to dinner when this was over. There was room at the house and room in her heart for them all. When she'd married Casey in Vegas she'd gained a mother-in-law, four brothers-in-law, a twenty-piece dinner set and a pet rescue hawk called Robin.

"If it's a girl we should call her Meadowlark," Rowan told Casey between pushes.

"We are not naming our daughter after Wyoming's state bird," muttered Casey. "What's taking so long?"

"And you were doing so well," said the midwife, prizing her hand out of Rowan's grip and checking the business end of dealings. "Okay, Tomas, help Rowan lean forward a little while you plump those pillows and make her as comfortable as possible. Hands around the backs of your knees, Rowan. That's quite a grip you've got there, isn't it?"

"What about Ava for a girl's name?" She was sweaty and bare-ass naked and all modesty had fled hours ago.

"Ava could work." Casey tried plumping pillows and ended up settling in behind her, so she could lean back on him instead. "Or Cheyenne, which was where this all started. What if it's a boy?"

Of all the tests that had been done, they'd never asked to know the sex of the baby. They'd take whatever came and feel blessed. "If it's a boy we call it James, after your father. James Joseph," she said.

"Or Joseph James after *your* father," Casey countered. "Joe has worried about this baby enough for all of us."

Casey winced as Rowan reached for his hand again and squeezed, lost in the grip of a contraction. The crush of his hand wasn't quite as bad as being hung up on a bull, but it came mighty close.

"Honestly, guys, decide later," said the midwife. "Rowan, I need you to push. Push *now*."

Rowan pushed. Casey bowed his head and prayed.

Ten minutes and six lifetimes' worth of pushing later a baby boy drew his first breath and cried and Casey gave thanks.

He had ten fingers and ten toes and Rowan looked shattered, and never again were they doing this, Casey vowed. Once was enough.

"It gets easier," said the midwife, and maybe the woman was a mind reader. "I need to weigh him and check him out but I'll be quick and I'll only be ten feet away, and then your son will be back with you. Casey, you can come and hover if you want to."

"I'll stay right here." Resting his head gently against Rowan's and still holding her hand and his was the grip that now wouldn't let go. "He's got ten fingers and ten toes," Casey whispered. "He's probably going to be an accountant."

"He's a fine healthy boy," said the midwife, minutes later, and placed the baby skin to skin across Rowan's chest. "Rowan, you're doing so well. Placenta next, okay, and, Casey, before you ask *again*, no, there's no untoward bleeding."

Which, fair enough, might have been a question on his lips.

"Would you like me to tell the crowd in the waiting room that you have a son?" the midwife continued.

"We'd love you to tell the crowd out there that we have a healthy baby boy." There were wagers running as to gender. Jett and Mab were going to win big.

Casey had wanted a smiling Rowan and a trouble-free birth and beyond that he'd been easy. He knew boys. Then again, a doe-eyed girl with flyaway hair and a will like her mother's would have terrorized them all and he'd have been grateful. He touched his son's tiny, fern-like fingers and watched in wonder as the baby's fingers closed around his.

"Good grip," he murmured and Rowan laughed weakly.

"I know what you're thinking," she said. "But there'll be no bull riding for him for quite some time."

"You realize Mason's got a pair of crocheted miniature cowboy boots out there already? In blue and red stripes."

"Bring 'em on. Your family's support is overwhelming and I love them, even Mason—sometimes."

Casey grinned. The rift between him and Mason hadn't healed completely but they were making progress. Mason had been one of the first to arrive when Rowan had gone into labor and had since done countless airport runs as others had staggered in. "He's not so bad once you get to know him. Bit like your father. Is now a good time to tell you that my mother's out there crocheting a cream-colored baby cowboy hat? She's probably finished by now."

"Baby cowboy hats are awesome." Rowan looked down. "Oh, Tomas, look at him. He's so beautiful."

He looked. At the baby in her arms and the woman who meant the world to him. He pressed his lips to her temple. "I'm looking. And I'll never stop loving you."

She touched her lips to his, soft and gentle. "Let's do this again."

"Never."

"I'll wear you down."

A chorus of cheers, whoops and yee-haws sounded somewhere outside the room, and that was his family out there, all of them. He'd go out and introduce them to the newest addition soon enough, but not yet. He needed this time alone with his wife and newborn child.

"As long as I can keep you safe." Because that was the crux of it. He needed her safe and standing right beside him. "You're my heart."

Twenty minutes later, with his tiny son safely wrapped in a blanket and cradled in the crook of his arm, Tomas pushed through the door to the waiting room and every bit of conversation stopped.

"Rowan's resting and doing really well. There were no complications." His gaze found Joe's, the man who so rarely shared his thoughts but who'd been pacing for eighteen hours solid. "This is Joseph." He met his mother's eyes next. "Joseph James, after his grandfathers, and there's more." He looked for Mab and found him tucked up in the corner, completely outnumbered by cowboys but still determined to be there. "Joseph. James. Macallister. Casey. And he's ours."

The End

The American Extreme Bull Riders Tour

If you enjoyed *Casey*, you'll love the rest of the American Extreme Bull Riders Tour!

Book 1: *Tanner* by Sarah Mayberry

Book 2: *Chase* by Barbara Dunlop

Book 3: *Casey* by Kelly Hunter

Book 4: *Cody* by Megan Crane

Book 5: *Troy* by Amy Andrews

Book 6: *Kane* by Sinclair Jayne

Book 7: *Austin* by Jeannie Watt

Book 8: *Gage* by Katherine Garbera

Available now at your favorite online retailer!

You won't want to miss more by Kelly Hunter…

Montana Born Series
What a Bride Wants

What a Bachelor Needs

Jackson Brother Series
Book 1: **The Courage of Eli Jackson**

Book 2: **The Heart of Caleb Jackson**

Book 3: **The Downfall of Cutter Jackson**

The Fairy Tales of New York series
Pursued by the Rogue

Available now at your favorite online retailer!

About the Author

Accidently educated in the sciences, **Kelly Hunter** didn't think to start writing romances until she was surrounded by the jungles of Malaysia for a year and didn't have anything to read. Kelly now lives in Australia, surrounded by lush farmland and family. Kelly is a USA Today bestselling author, a three-time RITA finalist and loves writing to the short contemporary romance form.

For more from Kelly:
Visit her website at KellyHunter.co

Thank you for reading

Casey

If you enjoyed this book, you can find more from all our great authors at TulePublishing.com, or from your favorite online retailer.